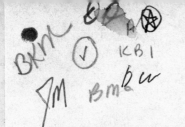

P9-CRC-849

# WAR ON ALKALI CREEK

Jack Farrell claimed to support the nesters in the range war against the cowmen, even though they thought he was turning against them. Day and night the air rang with the sound of guns spitting lead. Farrell was the only man who could stop the war, but only if he could hit harder and shoot faster than the men who had sworn to get him, and avert the inevitable full-scale slaughter . . .

# WAR ON ALKALI CREEK

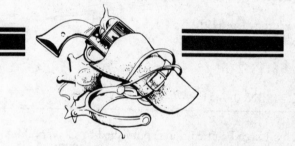

## Lee Floren

ATLANTIC LARGE PRINT
Chivers Press, Bath, England.
John Curley & Associates Inc.,
South Yarmouth, Mass., USA.

Library of Congress Cataloging in Publication Data

Floren, Lee.
  War on Alkali Creek / Lee Floren.
      p.    cm.—(Atlantic large print)
  ISBN 1–55504–822–6 (lg. print)
  1. Large type books.   I. Title.
[PS3511.L697W37 1989]
813'.52—dc19                                            88–7891
                                                          CIP

British Library Cataloguing in Publication Data

Floren, Lee, *1910–*
  War on Alkali Creek
  I. Title
  813'.52 [F]

  ISBN 0–7451–9470–2

This Large Print edition is published by Chivers Press, England, and
John Curley & Associates, Inc, U.S.A. 1989

Published by arrangement with Donald MacCampbell, Inc.

U.K. Hardback ISBN 0 7451 9470 2
U.S.A. Softback ISBN 1 55504 822 6

Copyright © 1951 by Phoenix Press
All rights reserved

# WAR ON ALKALI CREEK

899965

# CHAPTER ONE

The persistent knocking at the front door became louder. Finally the noise forced itself through the darkness of sleep. Jack Farrell sat up in bed and groped for a match to light the lamp.

Somebody was calling his name.

Still half asleep, Jack Farrell almost upset the chimney, but he grabbed it before it fell.

'Hold on a minute, fellow! Don't hammer down the door! Who's there?'

'Me, Sonny Doyle.'

Jack went to the door. 'What do you want at this hour of the night? Come on in.'

Sonny Doyle was sixteen and short and stocky. Lamplight reflected from unruly red hair.

'Somebody cut our ditch, Jack!'

Jack Farrell stopped in the act of pulling on a sock. 'Cut your ditch? The irrigation ditch out at your place, you mean? Which one?'

'The big one!'

Jack Farrell stood up now. He was twenty-five and six feet tall. He had thin hips that ran up to wide shoulders, and his face was square and full. 'Did you lose all the water out of your reservoir?'

'Danged near all of it, Jack.'

The youth's words had a dull edge of

1

despair. But still they possessed a certain harshness. While Jack finished dressing, the young farmer explained what had happened. He and his father had been irrigating their forty acres of alfalfa. They had set their turn-outs right and gone to bed, and Sonny had gone out at midnight to check the flow of water.

'An' when I got out to the main ditch, Jack, there was a big hole in it. Water was gushing out in a torrent. I ran up to the big-turn off and shut the flow off, but by that time most of the water had drained out of the reservoir.'

Jack Farrell looked at his gunbelt and holster, hanging from the peg on the hat rack. The lamplight reflected dully off the black butt of the single .45 that was pouched in the oily leather.

'You better take your gun, Jack.'

Jack said, 'Are you sure somebody cut that ditch, Sonny?'

Sonny swore with an anger that seemed incompatible with his sixteen years. 'I'm danged sure somebody cut that ditch. An' I'll tell you why, Jack. That ditch would never wash out, not with that small head of water forcin' it.'

'Muskrat?' Jack suggested.

Sonny knew what the irrigator meant. A muskrat has the habit of digging his den back into irrigation ditches. Sometimes he digs in

2

so far he weakens the ditch. When the ditch is filled, water trickles back into his den, and the result sometimes is that the ditch is washed out.

'Take your gun,' Sonny Doyle repeated. 'No muskrat hole caused that washout, Jack. For the simple reason that there were no muskrats in the ditch. You know that and so do I. We checked the ditch two days ago.'

'One might have swum into the ditch from the creek,' Jack said.

'You a-scared of these cowmen, Jack?'

Jack Farrell looked hard at the youth. But when he spoke he spoke almost quietly. 'Don't jump over your traces, kid. It might mean trouble for you and you know it. You say you're sure the cowmen cut your ditch. All right, have you got any evidence that either Milo Dawson or Ross Bassett cut that ditch?'

'What'd you mean by evidence? Ain't it a well-known fact neither of them cowmen wants us nesters here in this Wild River country? We all worked hard to fix the old man's farm for irrigation. Now, with water finally in our ditches, a ditch gets cut and we lose all our reservoir. And nobody knows when it'll rain again and fill it. What more evidence do you need?'

Jack figured he was wasting his time trying to explain to a sixteen-year-old kid who had his mind made up and in addition had a rough temper that matched his red hair. Sonny was right in some respects. Sonny's father—Mike Doyle—had worked hard at this farm and Jack Farrell had backed him with money. They had bought equipment and built a dam and made ditches. Now, with the first water going onto Doyle fields, the main ditch had gone out and with the water had gone the hopes of the Doyle clan. But still Sonny was on the wrong track, to some degree.

For the fact always remained the same: Milo Dawson was a cowman and Ross Bassett was a cowman, too. Dyed-in-the-wool cowmen who believed in open free range uncut by fence or furrow. Jack had tried to convince them their day was over. Maybe Martha Dawson—and the thought of her warm beauty—kept him from openly striking at either Dawson or Bassett.

'Did you see either of these cowmen cut that ditch?' Jack wanted to know.

'No . . . I didn't see 'em.'

Jack said, 'Then you're only acting on a guess, Sonny. To make a case stand up in court you have to have direct evidence. You haven't got it. Maybe a muskrat did cause that break-out. You don't know. You're only guessing. And guessing can get a man into a heap of trouble.'

'You afraid of them cowmen?'

'You know better than that.'

4

Sonny shrugged. 'A number of farmers aroun' here claim you kowtow to either Bassett or Milo Dawson.' The kid had the candor of undisciplined youth. 'I've heard quite a few of them say you was favorin' Milo Dawson because of his daughter. Some of us hoemen don't know whether you tricked us by gettin' us moved into Wild River or whether you're in earnest—'

Jack said, 'That's enough of that lip, kid. You've said plenty. If you was twenty-one, I'd knock you flat. Now get out to the barn and saddle my horse and I'll meet you in a minute or two.'

Sonny looked at him for a long moment. Jack wondered what thoughts the young face held. Sonny Doyle lifted his shoulders, and he seemed to have a bad taste in his mouth. He turned and went out the back door.

Jack Farrell slid into his buckskin jacket. Sonny Doyle, fired by anger and disgust, had inadvertently told Jack something he had suspected for some time: that his farmers were talking behind his back and were secretly distrustful of him. And maybe they had justification for such unrest.

Jack had been raised in this Wild River Basin. His father had been a cowman, but when Jack had been eleven years old Martin Farrell had sold out to Milo Dawson, and the old man had moved into Wild City and started the Mercantile Store. He had sent

5

Jack out to Miles City to go to high school. When Jack had graduated the Old Man had asked, 'You want to go to college?'

'No.'

'Why not?'

'Look, Dad.' Jack had spoken evenly. 'I'm not a book-man; I know that by now. You're no springchicken no longer. I'm your only kid. Mother's been dead six years now.'

'Yes?'

'Well—' Jack had paused, looking out the window. 'Well, I like store work. I'm goin' back home to help you out.'

'You're the boss, son.'

Old Martin Farrell had died two years ago. Jack remembered himself and his father driving across the wide expanse of Wild River Basin, looking at the river green with cottonwood and boxelder trees, a ribbon cutting the basin in two parts. And Jack had said, 'This would make a lot of good farms, Dad.'

'Not farms, son.' Old Martin had shaken his head firmly. 'This is no land for a plow. This is cow-country. God meant it for that, and cow-country it'll be until Gabriel does his trumpet work.'

Jack had said no more. Old Martin was a cowman through and through. But Jack had taken an agricultural course in high school, and he and his class had once made a field-trip down the Yellowstone River to

6

where a farmer had built a dam in the hills, compounded run-off rain water, and had a half-section of river-bottom under irrigation.

That trip had changed Jack's perspective on a number of things, and convinced him of several points. Chief of these was the fact that water, once applied to good Montana soil, could raise almost any crop. He had stood there and looked at the water trickling through the ditches and he had suddenly envisioned that green alfalfa field on Wild River. Wild River had hundreds of thousands of acres, and those acres, if irrigated—

He had not told this to Martin Farrell. Once or twice he had mentioned that if settlers came into Wild River Basin the Mercantile would boom, for it was the only store in miles. But his Old Man had said he had enough trade as it was, for the two big cow outfits bought all their supplies from him.

'This is good land,' Jack had said.

His father had glanced at him queerly. 'Good land for cattle,' Martin Farrell had finished.

Right after the Old Man had passed on, a stranger had registered at the Wild River House, the town's old hotel. This was the dull season—for the big cow outfits bought most of their supplies in early spring and late fall—and Jack had driven the stranger around the basin.

7

The man had often stopped the team, got out of the buckboard and dug into the soil. He had even put specimens of soil in small jars. For three days Jack had driven him around the basin, and his wonder had increased each day.

The man gave no clue as to his work. Finally Jack had asked, 'Mister, if it isn't Hoyle, don't answer my questions—but are you interested in the chances of successful farming here on Wild River?'

The man had said, 'It needs water.'

'We got water,' Jack told him. 'We can dam up a number of cricks—Beaver, Porcupine, Boxelder, Clear Crick—and we could build ditches and irrigate. This soil will raise anything in reason to the short growing season here. All it needs is water.'

'How do you know?'

'I've experimented.'

Jack had been using the warehouse and the backyard for an experimental farm. He had shown the man his work. The man had then disclosed he was an advance agent for the Montana Pacific Railroad and had been sent to Wild River to scout the possibilities of farming.

'Good wheat country,' Jack had said. 'It'll raise good barley and oats and any head-crop that will ripen in a reasonable length of time. Alfalfa grows mad if it gets water.'

'So I see from your experimental farm.'

There had been a silence. Finally the man had asked, 'And how about these two cowmen—Milo Dawson and Ross Bassett? I judge they won't want farmers in this country. Would they fight them?'

'I don't know.'

The man had said, 'They're cowmen, fellow. They've got hired cowpunchers who hate a farmer and what he stands for. In fact, they're holding back the development of the West.'

'They can't see that,' Jack had said.

The man had laid his cards on the table. So far the Montana Pacific had built to Cody Point, some seventy miles to the east, right inside the Dakota border. From there the railroad would either go up the Missouri and then the Milk Rivers, both to the north, or it would forge straight ahead into Wild River Basin, and meet the Missouri at Great Falls.

'We've got to get that railroad into Wild City,' Jack had said.

'Then you have to move in farmers and settle them. Because if the railroad builds in it has to make money, and it can't make money moving cattle twice a year for Dawson and Bassett. It has to move out produce—and lots of it—wheat, corn, barley, hay, and farm products.'

'This land is government land,' Jack had assured him. 'It's open for homesteading. You send on the farmers and I'll locate them.'

9

'You get five dollars per family.'

'I don't want the money. I want to make this country go ahead. For years cattle have held it back.'

Something about the enthusiasm in Jack Farrell's voice caused the railroad official to scowl. 'These cowmen won't give in without a fight, Mr. Farrell. I'll have to warn prospective settlers what awaits them in Wild River Basin if they take up homesteads.'

'Let's talk with Milo Dawson and Ross Bassett.'

They had held the conference in the office of the Mercantile. Both cowmen were wary and suspicious, not only of Jack and the railroad official, but also of each other.

Milo Dawson was the older by almost three decades, for Ross Bassett had been only a shave-tail button when he had started his Triangle S outfit on the north side of Wild River. He was a short, thick man, this Bassett, and he carried his authority plainly; it was a wide scarf around his heavy shoulders. He rodded a tough crew and boasted there wasn't a man in his crew he couldn't whip with his fists or a gun. He'd been called on this and each time he'd won.

Now he sat in his chair, dark eyes darting around the room. Milo Dawson, slender, grayhaired, sat across the room, his gaunt body slumped in his chair slightly. And beside him had sat his daughter, Martha.

Jack had leaned forward, elbows on his desk, apparently looking at a paper on the desk-top. Secretly, he had been watching Martha. She and he had played hide-and-seek together at the old schoolhouse. Then he had gone out to high school, and when he'd come back for good there had been a new Martha. Curves had taken the place of scrawniness. Pleasing curves, applied at the proper places. And her hair was even more golden, the yellow lamplight making it shimmer each time she moved her lovely head.

The railroad official had broached his plan, and instantly Milo Dawson and Ross Bassett had been against it. Jack had listened, seeing their side fully. They had run off the Indians, killed off the buffalo, and had run their cattle on Wild River grass. They had fought for their range with short-guns and rifles, and men had died for grass.

Now they were being asked to give up their range peacefully. Give it up to the westward march of an empire. Men had sat on soft seats in Congress—fat, pompous men—and they had passed an act called the Homestead Act. Any citizen could file on a quarter-section of land—one hundred and sixty acres—and in addition he could take up a desert-claim of half a section and sometimes a hill-claim of another quarter. This way, in many cases, his government gave him a mile of land—a section of free land.

Now Jack Farrell, buttoning his jacket, went out the back door into the moonlit night, and he remembered that meeting in his office. He remembered watching Milo Dawson and Ross Bassett. Dawson had listened, mouth opened slightly, but Ross Bassett had been a dark, secretive ball of a man, compact and tough and holding his thoughts. And then the railroad official had finished.

And there had been a silence, a heavy, thick silence, and Jack Farrell had felt its cold, ugly weight. And he knew then what the answer would be. He had really known that answer all the time.

'We don't need settlers,' Milo Dawson had rasped.

'No room for them,' Ross Bassett had growled.

Neither cowman tipped his hand. For once they were united against a common foe. Jack noticed neither had said he would fight nesters were they moved in. Neither was going on record as threatening the prospective farmers.

Dawson had said, 'Come on, Martha. A man can only stand so much of this nonsense.' He took his daughter's hand. She glanced at Jack, and later Jack wondered what her eyes had held. Had they held pity or fear for him?

Ross Bassett had come to his boots, stocky

and tough. He had looked at Jack and asked bluntly, 'Where do you stand, Farrell?'

Jack had said, 'My father was a cowman—'

Bassett got the wrong impression. He cut in with, 'Once a cowman, always a cowman. I appreciate your stand, Farrell. I was afraid you were with this railroad man.'

'You never let me finish.'

They had stopped then and stood there and looked at him. Milo Dawson, shaggy, old, still rawhide, stood wide-legged, and Martha, the lamplight lost in her blond hair, looked at him, too. And Ross Bassett stood there, eyes narrowed now.

'Go ahead—finish—'

Jack had said, 'I'm for bringing in farmers.'

Martha had said, 'Jack—' Then she had stopped. She had watched him, and he saw her teeth come down and crush her pretty lip.

'You mean that, Jack?' Milo Dawson's voice was hollow and he seemed to doubt his ears.

But Ross Bassett had said huskily, ''Course he means it! Didn't he tote this railroadman all over the country? He's behin' this, too. What would the Old Man Farrell say if he was here—?'

'That's enough!'

Jack had spoken quietly, yet danger lay beneath his words. And Ross Bassett had let his right hand settle on the pearl-handled grip

13

of the big Colt .45 in his hand-tooled holster.

But the railroad man had come in between them. 'Don't jump on Farrell,' he had warned. 'I only hired him to drive me around! I'm behind this and I represent Montana Pacific—'

'A thievin' outfit,' Bassett had snorted. 'Come on, Milo.'

They left, and Jack and the railroad man had looked silently at each other. Then the railroad official had said, 'You made an enemy, Jack.'

Jack nodded. 'He's hated me for years. Ever since I was a kid, he hated me. He hated the Old Man, too. He's got no friends.' He walked to his desk, drummed long fingers on the rim. 'You move settlers in, Mr. Johnson, and I'll locate them. We'll incorporate and make an irrigation system. Will the railroad give us any financial support?'

'I don't know.'

'Find out if they will. Let me know by return mail.'

But as it turned out, the Montana Pacific had no money to invest in an irrigation scheme that might not pan out. By fall they would stop grade construction and hole up in Cody Point for the winter. If Jack could have settlers located by fall—enough farmers on homesteads—they would drive rails through the Wild River country. And Jack had told Johnson to send in settlers.

So they had come in. They had shipped by rail to the end of steel, then unloaded wagons and cattle and supplies and their families and continued west by wagons. They were all, it seemed, a little stunned by the immensity of this land. Jack realized the land must have seemed terribly unfriendly to them. For the land was dry, the grass burned down by the sun, and the only timber was back in the mountains or along the river and creeks.

They came from Pennsylvania and Indiana and Ohio and Illinois. One family came from North Carolina. They had some money of their own, but this was not much, for a money panic was on and the land they had sold back east had not drawn much. They were, in a sense, refugees.

Many of them had farmed rented land. They were all hungry for a new start and a chance to work and prosper. Jack had located them along creeks, helped them all he could, and when winter had come they had all been somewhat settled. Maybe not too comfortably settled, but settled just the same.

Ross Bassett had said, 'This winter'll drive 'em out. Ever look at the winter coats on the cows an' horses? I seen a yearlin' bull over on the Big Warm last week that had a real coat on hisself. When a cow or horse grows hair like they're doin' now, it means a whamdinger of a hard winter ahead.'

'They'll be there in the spring,' Jack had

15

assured him.

Bassett had measured him with a cold calculating look. 'I can't quite understand you, Farrell. Your daddy was a cowman, and he played ball with me an' Milo Dawson. By all rights of blood and training, you should be against the settlers. Yet here you're movin' 'em in.'

'You can't hold this country.'

Bassett's thick forefinger had tapped his holster suggestively. 'There's no law here except what a man makes, Farrell. The county never even stationed a deputy here in Wild City. Might makes right here, an' us cowmen have the might.'

'You're running against your own government.'

Bassett shook his head. 'Them boys in Washington passed the Homestead Act, sure. But they had pressure on them from the big harvesting machinery manufacturers. They ain't worried one whit about Wild River Basin.'

The cowman's prophecy had proven correct. For winter howled down and dealt death. Snow covered fence posts and snow drifted roads shut. Farmers ran ropes between their houses and their barns and chicken coops. They followed these ropes. Otherwise they'd have been lost in the blizzards that swept across this high range country.

Some had cut hay along the bottoms, bluejoint hay and foxtail. And some had cut down buckbrush for food. Cows and horses ate it all. Out on the range cowboys rode gaunt, wind-broken horses. Cowboys were muffled to their ears in scarfs and cowboys wore overshoes and heavy woolen pants under thick angora chaps. They cut cows open and found in their cold bellies hunks of wild rosebush and buckbrush the size of a man's fist.

Both Milo Dawson and Ross Bassett lost lots of cattle. Cattle that died in snow-drifts. Cattle drifted with the storm, came to the fences of nesters, and there they piled up and died. The farmers pulled most of their stock through, but the two cowmen had losses up to thirty percent.

Milo Dawson had said, 'Them nesters cost me lots of stock. My cattle drifted into their fences and froze there and piled up. If them fences hadn't been there, they'd have reached timber and chawed down branches and buckbrush.'

'You should put up hay,' Jack had pointed out.

'Ain't never run a mower, an' I'm too old to start now.'

Jack looked at Martha.

Martha had said, 'Jack's right, Dad. Cut hay in the draws and stack it for next winter. The farmers never lost many cattle.'

'You playin' fiddle for them homesteaders now, girl?'

Martha had colored. 'Dad, keep a civil tongue.'

Old Milo had stomped out of the Mercantile. Outside, spring had finally arrived. Grass was shooting up under the warm sun.

Jack said, 'Thanks, Martha.'

'Don't thank me, Jack Farrell. You got yourself into this mess; I didn't. I hear you intend to build dams and irrigate.'

'We plan that.'

'You got any money?'

'Not much,' he admitted ruefully.

Martha had said, 'You'll break the Merc, Jack. And your dad worked hard to build this business. I understand Ross Bassett is threatening to put up a store of his own and run competition to you. Bassett says you can deal with the nesters and he'll deal with the cowboys.'

'That's just talk.'

'It might not be.'

'I think it is, Martha. Bassett doesn't know the mercantile business.' Jack felt a little out of sorts. Martha was too close to him, for one thing. He never had been much of a hand with the girls. For one thing, he'd worked too hard to have time to chase around; for another, he had more or less made up his mind that Martha was the one. Not that he

18

had ever mentioned it to anybody, not even his Old Man when the Old Man had been alive.

'Jack.'

'Yes?'

'Jack, I don't like this. Personally, I think you're right.'

Jack had said, 'Thanks, Martha.'

It had taken nerve to say that. She was old Milo Dawson's only child. Her mother had been sickly for years and Martha had been practically the only woman on the big cow outfit. She was the same as saying her father was wrong, and Jack knew how the golden-haired girl admired Milo Dawson.

'I don't know—Jack I'm afraid for you.'

It had happened then. Afterwards Jack tried to remember it all, but he couldn't because the lines were not clear. But a girl had been in his arms and he had kissed her very clumsily.

Then both were laughing, for no apparent reason at all.

## CHAPTER TWO

The darkness was breaking into a gray dawn. Jack Farrell stood on the ditch and looked at the break. He saw mud and silt and a break about twenty feet wide in the ditch.

'It can be patched,' Mike Doyle said. 'After it dries I can get in there with a team and a slip and scrape up a new bank.'

Mike Doyle was an older replica of Sonny Doyle. Stocky, heavy-chested, he was a regular farmer and a good farmer. His battered old black hat was shoved back and showed red hair.

His square face that sported a week's growth of whiskers could not hide his disappointment, though. Nor could the ready grin on his sun-blackened lips hide the anger and discontentment rolling inside the farmer.

'Wonder how it happened?' Mike Doyle asked.

Jack walked up and down the dike. Many footprints showed here. He also saw the tracks of horses. That was only logical. The Doyles kept walking along the top of the bank while irrigating, going from one turn-out to another. Also, they sometimes rode along the dike going to the north pasture for the milk-cows.

Jack knew that the tracks could tell nothing. It might be that either Bassett or Milo Dawson had cut the dike or ordered one of their cowboys to sneak in under cover of night and cut the bank. For a narrow cut in the dike would soon widen when water whipped through it. The bank was new and soft and therefore it had washed out easily. Jack looked at the alfalfa field.

20

The alfalfa was not damaged much. That close to the break had been washed out by the force of the water. Mud and silt covered some of it, but this was only for a short distance in front of the break.

Jack smiled wanly. 'Anyway, it got plenty of water, huh, Mike?'

'That it did,' Mike Doyle said. 'The alfalfa will straighten up again, but the reservoir is empty.'

'Might rain,' Jack said.

They all looked to the sky. Not a cloud in sight. Westward the mountains were high, reaching like thick fingers into the heavens, already lighted at their peaks by the rising sun, still hidden to Jack Farrell and the farmer and his son, for they were in the natural depression of Wild River Basin.

Not a cloud around the top of the highest peak, even though snow still glistened there in the crags. By fall that snow would be gone. It would be melted and would have run off in the form of water. But the ironical thing was that that snow-water would not run down into Wild River Basin. Most of it—almost all of it—would trickle into creeks that ran to the west and drained into the Snow River across the ridge.

Not a cloud either overhead or to the east. For months the summer had dragged on without any rain. Spring's sun had melted the snow and it had run off, making the creeks and river mad with flood water. Farmers had drilled in wheat and head-crops and these had sprouted quickly. Head-crops had pushed upward out of the strong earth, used up the sub-moisture, and now they stood silent and brown, seemingly begging for rain.

Unless rain came, grain-crops would be ruined. One more rain would fill out heads, and then the sun would mature the wheat and barley. Corn was doing pretty well, for corn needed very little moisture. Corn would be the only crop that would pay, unless rain came.

And without rain, the reservoir could not be refilled. Jack and the Doyles had labored hard and long to make this irrigation system. First, they had built the dam in the hills. They had hired farmers and laborers and had built the dam with fresnoes and had put a rock face and tail on it. They had built rock and concrete turn-outs and had run two main canals to the dam, angling them along the edge of the hills.

This would be the model for future irrigation systems. The Doyles had invested almost all of their small savings and Jack had spent more money than he cared to admit. To look at his books in the Mercantile almost made him shudder. His cash reserve was very low . . . too low.

For one thing, he carried both Milo Dawson and Ross Bassett during spring roundup, for the cowmen paid their bills once a year—and that payment came after cows had been driven to the railhead, shipped into either the Chicago or Minneapolis slaughter-pens. Both cowmen had run big crews during calf roundup, for the blizzard had scattered cows back in the foothills.

The farmers had tried, the fall before, to negotiate loans from the Interior Department in Washington; their government had turned them down. Jack had also tried to borrow money off the railroad, but no dice. The railroad officials were playing cards close to their chests. With a money panic tying up loose change, they needed every cent they had . . . or so they claimed.

Jack had summed it up neatly. 'Then you're putting me and my farmers on our own? Is that it? You're cutting us off altogether?'

The pompous official had coughed and hemmed and hawed. He had his stockholders to think about, his company—he had this and that. Jack saw further argument was useless. He had ridden back to Wild City, coming in on the twice-a-week stage. And while crossing the wide basin, again his dream had taken form and shape.

He wasn't wrong. His farmers were not wrong. Deserted by their government and the railroad, they would fight on. To a man, each farmer had everything he owned invested in his land, his livestock, his buildings. They and Jack were together, close to the end of their financial ropes, and they'd have to fight this through together.

But some of the farmers, Jack knew, were getting frightened. He carried them on his books for their household supplies. As long as the wholesale houses carried him and his Mercantile Store, they would eat, but if the wholesalers got scared and demanded payment—

Jack didn't like to think of that.

Jack climbed the gully and looked at the reservoir. Not much irrigation water left, he saw; this made a wry taste across his mouth. If Dawson or Bassett had cut that dike they had done a good job of running the reservoir down. Mike Doyle panted from the climb.

'What'd you say, Jack?'

'You got water enough to irrigate about twenty acres, I'd say. If I were you I'd put it on my wheat. Get that wheat into good heads and we'll harvest it, and it'll pull you through next year maybe.'

'Maybe.'

Jack detected the farmer's sourness.

'They goin' get rails in here by fall?' Mike Doyle asked. 'Or do we have to haul what little crops we got to Cody Point?'

'I thought you'd heard, Mike. The money panic back in Wall Street has closed down Montana Pacific's grade-building. Johnson dropped me a line the other day telling me the work had stopped until money loosens up again.'

'When will it loosen?'

'Ask some big Wall Street banker,' Jack said.

Mike Doyle rubbed his whiskery chin. 'We're behin' the cue ball, all right. Now the big shots has tied up the railroad. I wonder if it is money that stopped grade-buildin', Jack.'

'I don't follow you.'

Doyle spread work-gnarled hands. 'Those road officials are playin' it close to their chests. They still don't know whether they'll run up the Missouri River, or if'n they'll cut across Wild River Basin. Me, I don't think it's the money panic so much that's tyin' them up. I think they're layin' aroun' watchin' us farmers. If we make good this year, rails come through Wild River; if we flop and have to pull out, rails go north along the Big Muddy.'

Jack gave this proposition serious thought. He had come to the same conclusion a few weeks ago, but he gave the impression this idea was new to him. Mike Doyle's ego was rather low and it needed a boost.

'You got something there, Mike. I'd not connected those two in my mind yet. But still, it spells the same thing to you and me—we can't do nothing, can we?'

'We can wring the necks of Dawson and

Bassett!'

Jack told the father the same thing he had told Sonny. They had no evidence pointing toward either of the cowmen as being the instigators of this ditch-cutting. But Mike Doyle also had a tough temper. He shook his head doggedly, stubborn to his Irish core.

'I catch one of them—or one of their cowhands—hangin' aroun' here, Jack, an' I might be apt to salt him down with a Winchester.'

'Catch them or their men doing anything to your property,' Jack reminded him, 'and you've got right to defend yourself and your holdings. But you know full well what'll happen if you get a rifle and go out cowman hunting, don't you?'

Seriousness caught the whiskery face. 'That would be a bad idea, Jack. You're right. Fact is, a man might get killed; another fact, the other farmers would be pulled into it, too. And gunsmoke would be the result.'

'That's straight thinking,' Jack said.

'Come on up to the shack for a cup of coffee, Jack?'

Jack said, 'Heck, I haven't even had breakfast yet.'

They went to the homestead shack. Mrs. Doyle was a dark-haired, thin woman with a work-worn appearance. Jack Farrell found himself thinking she looked more tired than she should have. Then he decided she was not so haggard from work as she was from worry.

Thinking back, he remembered that same frightened, wearied look on other farmer-wives—on Mrs. Mayhenry, Mrs. Schell, Mrs. Pasco, and the other farmer-women. And, in a minor way, Martha's face reflected a similar worry.

That thought held no happiness for him. He tried to bury it, but it kept popping back into his memory with its sourness. Mrs. Doyle had hotcakes and coffee ready. Her oldest girl helped her while the youngest girl and the baby sat on the bed, watching them.

'How many farmers are there now, Mr. Farrell?' the woman wanted to know.

'An even dozen.'

'Any more coming in?'

'Not that I know of,' Jack answered. 'The railroad has quit recruiting back east, you know. They're watching us to see if we prosper.'

'We need rain, and lots of it.'

Jack pointed out that dry-land farming was no good here. About one crop in ten years, he figured. 'We have to have water at the right time, and that means dams.'

'If somebody doesn't cut your ditches you're all right,' the woman said.

Jack was glad to get outside again. He didn't like to argue with a man, and argument with a woman was worse than wasted. Mrs. Doyle hadn't been in a very civil humor. Not that he blamed her any, at that. She had justification for pessimism.

'We'll have to fix that ditch,' Mike Doyle said.

Jack got his horse and rode back toward Wild City. His trip out here had been almost useless. There had been nothing he could have done. The damage had been done and that was that. He was pretty sure either Milo Dawson or Ross Bassett had ordered the dike cut.

As Sonny had said, they had patrolled the ditch carefully, looking for muskrat holes that could develop into breaks in the dike. And they had found none. Nor had too much water in the dike washed it out. The high-water mark had been too low for that, Jack had noticed.

No, the dike had been cut. Then, with water rushing through to freedom, the breach had widened. And the only ones who would cut the dike, or want the dike cut, would be the two Wild River Basin cowmen.

Jack built up the scene in his mind. A man, coming through the night, packing a shovel. A man digging like mad into the new, soft bank. Then the gurgle of water trickling to freedom—a gurgle that must have suddenly increased into the mad leap of free water.

That was a low way to fight. Hitting in the night, fighting a poor family trying to get their talons into the soil and hang on until

28

they were established. Could a man get lower than that?

Jack found himself doubting it.

Because of the lowness of the act, it hardly seemed possible that Milo Dawson had ordered the dike cut. Dawson was of the old cowman school and he always fought in the open. Dawson and Jack's father had been old friends. Jack found himself thinking, I don't think Milo Dawson had that dike cut.

Or did he think thus because of Martha Dawson? He knew that, because of Martha, he had a soft spot in his heart for old Milo. Not that the old devil needed any sympathy. He was gruff and bluff, but Martin Farrell had many times said, 'Ol' Milo'd give a man the shirt off'n his back.'

His thoughts switched to Ross Bassett. He felt sure that Bassett would play such a dirty game under cover of night. Bassett was dark and secretive and the man was a fighter. Time had somewhat dulled the blade of old Milo Dawson's temper and greed. But Bassett was still strong and with enough of his youth left to fire him with greediness and desire for power.

But his thoughts, he realized, were darting wildly around and accomplishing nothing. He swung his bronc south and an hour later rode into the yard of a farmhouse set beside Beaver Creek. The log house's unpealed logs, new and shiny, glistened in the sun.

A woman carried out a pail of slop-water, threw it into the creek. Jack asked, 'Where's Bob?'

'Up to the dam, Mr. Farrell. Him an' Schell an' Mayhenry an' Sherman is up there workin'. How goes things with you?'

'Fine.'

'Good luck somebody's gittin' along good.' Mrs. Pasco went into the house where the baby was crying. Jack rode up the creek, following a well-traveled wagon-trail. Bob Pasco and his neighbors were building a dam in Beaver Creek. It would be even bigger than the dam he and Mike Doyle had built. Also, Beaver Creek ran most of the year; therefore the dam would always store up water.

Beaver Creek was pretty low right now. The drought had dried up some of the big springs that fed the stream. Jack saw the back of a carp sticking out of the water in the stillness behind a big rock. The carp was laying eggs in the sand. He and Martha used to come up behind the big fish, years ago, and spear them. Martha had become a good hand at the job.

Jack rode into a narrow defile that had brush and rock on either side. A man came out of the buckbrush with a rifle. Jack said, 'Heck of a way to greet a friend, Bob Pasco.'

Bob Pasco was a well-built man with a ready smile. 'We've got to play our cards close, Jack. What d'you know for certain?'

'Not much. How's the dam coming?'

'Look it over, huh?'

They were building the dam right around the bend. They had built a coffer-dam and they had blasted out the side of the rock and through this they had run Beaver Creek. This way they could work unhampered to build the dam across the original bed of the stream.

They squatted on the bank—Jack, Bob Pasco, Mayhenry and Schell. Pasco had studied to be a civil engineer and had not completed his schooling; still, he knew a lot about dam construction.

'We're doin' the slow work now,' Pasco explained. 'Notice we built a dirt core to our dam. Now we're haulin' in rock for the face and tail of it. Then, when it's complete, spillway and all, we'll put a little powder in that cliff and close the channel we made.'

'Ought to have concrete to face and tail with,' Jack reminded him. 'Should make that spillway out of concrete, too.'

'Where we goin' get the dinero to buy cement?' Bob Pasco sounded disgusted. 'Cement sells for thirty some cents a sack down at Cody Point. And where we goin' get the dinero to buy it?'

'Will rock hold it?' Jack asked.

'Has to hold it. We'll put fine gravel between the rock. That'll help, too. Yeah, it's gotta hold, Jack.'

They talked of other things. Finally Jack

told them about the dike breaking on the Mike Doyle farm. 'Lost almost all the water in his reservoir too,' Jack finished.

Mayhenry said, 'Who cut the dike?'

Jack said, 'Maybe it wasn't cut.'

Pasco spat into the stream. 'One of them cowmen cut it, Jack. I looked it over before water was turned into it. Doyle let water in slow and let it soak for two days before he turned his head of irrigation water into it. That dike went out because of a shovel workin' on it, I'll say.'

'What can we prove?' Jack wanted to know.

Pasco spat again. 'Nothin', per usual.'

Mayhenry and Schell were silent, and Jack guessed at their thoughts. From now on an armed guard would guard this dam night and day. Jack got to his feet. 'I'd try to get you some cement, men, but it'd be no use. My wholesale house wouldn't trust me that far.'

'That close, huh?' Pasco asked.

'Nip and tuck.'

Pasco said, 'We'd best get to work, Jack. This dam ain't buildin' itself.' His gaze was level. 'Guard night and day out here from now on.'

'One reason I rode over,' Jack reminded him.

Jack rode back down the defile. When he reached open range for some reason he felt a little better. Maybe it was because the canyon had been like his thoughts: confining, hemming him in, blocking him.

He met Martha a mile this side of town. She wore cream-colored buckskin—a split riding-skirt, a buck-skin jacket over a white silk blouse. Her hat lay on her back, held by the throat-strap, and the sunlight found her hair and liked it. She rode a black-and-gray pinto—a gaudy, flashy gelding forever rolling the cricket in his bit.

Jack joshed, 'Going into town for a spool of thread?'

'How did you guess it?'

'You mean that?'

She laughed, and he liked it. 'Yes, silly, I mean it. Number forty, white. You got a spool in your so-called store?'

'That's about all I have left,' Jack said.

She caught the soberness of his voice. And it drew a slight frown across her tanned high forehead.

'What's wrong, Jack?'

He told about the break in Mike Doyle's main canal and the loss of the farmer's irrigation water.

'Did the ditch break?'

'I think it was cut.'

He gave her a quick glance, half hoping her face would show something. Surely if her father had ordered the canal cut she would know something about it. But her face showed only genuine shock. He was sure of that.

'Who would cut it?'

'Either Ross Bassett,' he said, 'or your father.'

'Jack, that's hitting below the belt!'

He felt a surge of anger. He knew his tongue was getting away from his logic, but he said it nonetheless.

'Somebody sure hit Mike Doyle below the belt!'

She said, 'Let's not quarrel. The day is too nice, Jack.'

'It isn't nice for the farmers,' he pointed out.

She turned in saddle, hand on fork and horn. 'Jack, you shouldn't have moved them in. Now the drouth is here after that terrible winter last winter, and, Jack, they blame you. You know that.'

'We'd make it, if it wasn't for the cowmen. Where does your father stand in this, Martha?'

Anger made her face even more lovely. He saw her teeth crush her bottom lip, and he heard the fast hiss of her breathing.

'You ask him,' she snapped.

Then she put spurs to her pinto and loped ahead. He did not follow. He kept his horse at its running-walk. Maybe he had been wrong; maybe he had been right. Anyway, she had no reason to fly off the handle. Or had she?

Gradually his thoughts tightened and regained clarity. He remembered her awed expression when he had told her about the dike being broken. If Milo Dawson had ordered the Doyle dike cut, then Dawson had kept the order secret from his daughter. And that was only logical, Jack Farrell figured.

Old Milo Dawson was not one to tip his hand, even to his daughter. He was a cowman of the old school and he could be ruthless when and if the occasion demanded. He would not tell Martha he aimed to break Doyle's dike.

But still, the odds pointed towards Ross Bassett.

## CHAPTER THREE

Jack Farrell stabled his bronc in the barn back of his house. He unsaddled and slipped off the animal's bridle and put a hackamore on him and tied him to the manger. Then he doled hay in through the hay-window and went into the house.

Tomorrow the cleaning-woman would come in, but now the place looked like typical bachelor quarters. To save his soul he couldn't keep a house clean. He crammed some dry twigs into the stove and warmed up some coffee. It was old and rancid, but he drank it anyway.

Somebody knocked on the back door.

'Come in.'

The kid was about ten, barefooted and with knee pants. 'Ma sent me over to look for you, Jack. The freighter just come in with some supplies from Cody Point. I been lookin' for you for about an hour.'

'What does your mother want?'

'She don't know where you want the stuff placed in the warehouse. Most of it is salt-blocks for them danged cowmen.'

'Be right over, Bill.'

Bill Stebbins left. Jack finished his coffee, smiling at the boy's words: *for them danged cowmen*. Bill had been playing with the kids of the farmers and had evidently picked up a few of their expressions.

The Cody Point freighter had two wagon-loads full of supplies. He had his teams and wagons behind the Merc in front of the warehouse, which fronted the alley. When Jack arrived the man was squatting in the shade of a wagon-wheel talking with one of the town pensioners, a garrulous oldster who always had lots of gossip.

'Done heered somebody cut Doyle's ditch?' the old pensioner said, peering up at Jack, his goatee working up and down as he chewed finecut.

''Pears that way,' Jack admitted.

'Good,' the old man chortled. 'Oughta run

them farmers out, they should. Good for the cowmen.'

Jack winked at the freighter. 'He gets a pension from the Rafter T. That's why he's so behind the cowmen.'

'Cowmen built this country,' the pensioner maintained.

The freighter got to his feet. 'I think you're wrong, Septimus. The cowmen never built this country: Gawd built it. Now get to work unloading this block-salt and these supplies. I gotta get goin' back an' make Soda Springs for tonight's camp.'

'We still ain't settled on a wage yet,' Septimus reminded him.

'Ten cents an hour. My limit.'

'Fifteen cents.'

The freighter shrugged. 'My limit, fella.'

Septimus spat and walked off. Jack said, 'He don't want to work; he just wants to argue. I'll get help out to you right after I show you where I want this stuff unloaded.'

'Letter come along with this freight,' the freighter said. 'Glued onto a package. I took it loose so it wouldn't get lost.' He handed Jack Farrell the letter, and Jack noticed it came from the wholesale house that had shipped out his supplies. He went into his store, entering through the back door. Mrs. Stebbins was waiting on a customer, and that customer turned out to be Martha Dawson.

Jack said, 'See you got into town safe,

Martha.'

'Thank you.'

Jack smiled, went into his office and found his chair. He leaned back, looking through the glass that enclosed him. He had an idea what that letter contained. Finally he ripped it open.

His surmise had been right. The wholesale house asked if he couldn't pay up seventy-five percent of his account. That was something new. Heretofore he had paid once a year, after the bills of the Rafter T and the Triangle S had been paid in the fall.

He understood.

Somehow the wholesaler had gotten word that things were not progressing just right in Wild River Basin. He was getting afraid for his money. Probably he had communicated with Jack's banker in Cody Point and got a statement from him anent the financial condition of one Jack Farrell who operated the Mercantile, the only general store in the inland town of Wild City.

'Nice old banker,' Jack thought sourly. 'Thanks, old friend, thanks.'

Mrs. Stebbins was wrapping up Martha's purchases. Martha's gaze met Jack's. She jerked her eyes away. He hardly noticed. He was busy thinking about debts and not about a lovely golden-haired hothead. He wadded up the letter and it slammed into his wastepaper basket so hard it bounced out again. He left it on the floor.

When Mrs. Stebbins came in, he was looking at his account-book with that particular wholesaler.

'You forgot to pay me yesterday, Mr. Farrell.'

Jack said, 'Ouch.'

'Is—money that close?'

Jack smiled. 'Forgive me, Nellie.' He opened his safe and counted out her wages. 'I'm getting old and stubborn and forgetful, I guess.'

'If you need money bad, Jack, I can wait. I've got a little saved up, and there's just Billy and me now. Jimmy went into Cody Point to try to get work on the railroad.'

'They've shut down,' Jack said. 'The money panic.'

A customer entered and Nellie Stebbins left. Jack added up what he owed the wholesale house and then said to himself, You can wait, brother; you can wait. Maybe the wholesaler was hard up for dinero too and was caught in the money tieup in Wall Street. Maybe it wasn't because he had heard about this Wild River trouble.

The freighter came in. 'You got a reply to that letter?'

'No reply.'

The man had guessed correctly about the letter's contents. Evidently other stores he freighted had received similar letters.

'Maybe I won't see you for a while then, Jack.'

'Maybe not, fella. Good luck.'

The freighter left, and later Jack heard the two wagons leave. To save the expense of hiring another driver the freighter had his back team tied to the end-gate of the first wagon, which he drove. Jack thought, Looks like everybody is cutting expenses. Maybe he'd have to let Mrs. Stebbins go. No, he couldn't do that; she'd worked years for his father. She was a part of the Merc. Just as much a part of the store as the big lamp that you lowered down to light. Just as much a part of it as the familiar odor of dried prunes and the bolts of cloth and the groceries.

And if he did let her go, what would the woman do for a living? There was no other work for her here in this small town. Jack got to his feet and angrily dismissed the thought.

Young Bill Stebbins came in, flipping a quarter. 'Old tight-wad loosened up this time, Jack. 'Stead of givin' me a dime, that freighter gave me a quarter for helpin' him unload.'

'Maybe he was sick?'

'He must've been, to be that liberal.' Bill made the quarter twinkle; then it fell into his not too clean palm. 'Ross Bassett's in town. He's down at the Ace Up Bar, Jack.'

'Why tell me?'

Bill Stebbins looked away. 'Just thought

I'd tell you, Jack. Old Septimus told me Bassett was makin' talk. Seems as if he jumped a farmer out on the grass. Farmer hinted that mebbe Bassett had helped Doyle's dike along a little.'

Jack's blood quickened. 'What farmer did he jump?'

'Max Stanton, so Septimus said.'

Jack said, 'Thanks, kid.'

Bill gave him a glance, then went out the front door. But when he had walked past his mother, the quarter had made a shiny leap into Mrs. Stebbins palm. 'That's for us, Mom. In the old sock.'

So Ross Bassett had jumped Max Stanton . . . Stanton was an ex-clerk—a thin, stoop-shouldered man of about fifty—and he had spent his life and his eyes and his small strength in too many close offices. He had headed into Wild River Basin to make a home for himself and his elderly mother.

But in the sickly man was a fierce spark of self-reliance. Stanton had probably accused Ross Bassett of cutting the Doyle dike. His temper would make him reckless. And had Bassett fought with him?

That would be no fight. Not with Bassett stocky and confident and with hard knuckles. That would be no fight; that would be a slaughter.

Mrs. Stebbins hurried back, 'Jack, Mr. Bassett is coming this way.'

41

'He alone, Nellie?'

'He's got Slim Redden with him.'

Jack nodded, keeping calm. Redden was Bassett's range-boss. A slim, thin-faced man of uncertain age, with dull gray eyes and the habit of rubbing his long nose. But Redden, despite his wiriness, was tough. He rodded the Triangle S with a hard hand, and only last spring he had killed a cowhand who had pulled a gun on him. Redden didn't look tough. But he was tough.

The woman asked, 'What do you aim to do?'

'Wait for them.'

She said, 'I'll get over by the counter. Your shotgun is over there, under the counter.'

'Get next to it,' Jack said.

The shotgun was not loaded. Evidently she did not know this. If Bassett and Redden were coming toward the Merc, then they aimed to come into the Merc. Because the Merc was the last building in the block.

Jack was sitting at his desk, making a pretense of working, but all the time he heard the boots as they entered and came back toward his office. He looked up just as Ross Bassett stopped in the doorway.

Slim Redden stood behind his boss. A thin rope-scarred hand came up and slowly felt along the bridge of the long nose. Dull eyes looked at Jack Farrell, who took his gaze back to Ross Bassett.

42

'Something for you men?' Jack asked.

Bassett had had one drink too many, and drink had dulled the edges of his subtlety. He went straight to the point. 'I understand Mike Doyle's big ditch broke an' flooded his alfalfa and he lost most of the water out of his dam?'

Jack nodded. He looked at Slim Redden, and Redden did not look away. Neither did Ross Bassett, and Bassett's eyes were hot now.

'Anything else?' Jack wanted to know.

Bassett said, 'That sodbuster back yonder on Elk Crick—that Stanton—he accused me of cuttin' that dike. I slapped him around a little. I wouldn't dare hit him; I'd kill him.'

'So I heard,' Jack admitted.

Bassett was watching him. He had both hands down and his thumbs were hooked in his gunbelt. Jack Farrell was careful to keep his hands away from his own holstered gun. Bassett was fast with a gun; so was Slim Redden. He didn't want to die. Not right now, anyway.

'How come that dike broke, Farrell?'

Jack said, 'I don't know. It wasn't a muskrat digging into the bank. We checked the entire dike the other day. No muskrats had dug dens back into the soil. Doyle let it soak up good, and the head of water wasn't big enough to break it.'

'Then what busted it?' Ross Bassett was stubborn.

43

Jack said quietly, 'You figure that out.'

Bassett moved back. The Triangle S man looked at his foreman, and Jack saw the start of his cynical, secretive smile. He wanted to knock that smile off those thick lips, but he managed to hold his temper.

'You accusin' anybody?' Bassett demanded.

Jack said, 'You came looking for trouble.'

A townswoman came in to make a purchase, saw the three men talking, and then left again. Out on the street a rig moved with the sound of hoofs and the creak of the buckboard. Mrs. Stebbins' motherly face was the color of mauled clay. Her hands were under the counter.

Ross Bassett said, 'Maybe I did come for trouble, Farrell. But nobody's passin' aroun' accusations that me or my men is cuttin' irrigation ditches. You got these pun'kin-rollers in here and you're responsible for them. This is no farmin' country an' you know it.'

'Water'll make it a farming community.'

Bassett said, 'That's a bronc of another color. There's water, but it's wild, an' you an' your sodmen ain't got the equipment or money necessary to corral it. The handwritin' is there and some are readin' it. You see it, but you're like your old man—you're too stubborn.'

'Keep my dad out of this,' Jack warned.

For a moment harsh anger whipped across his face. It drew down his forehead and carved its rough imprint across his mouth. Then logic pushed this anger aside with slow stubbornness.

This pair had come here with the firm intent of angering him and driving him to action. Then they would kill him. He was sure of that. Ross Bassett was reckless, for this thing was shaping up, bringing with it its own climax. Now Bassett wanted to push this climax, for patience was just a word to him and not a trait of his character.

He looked beyond Ross Bassett and his eyes met Mrs. Stebbins'. And he saw the slow movement of the matron's head in negation. That also helped him regain his old composure.

He said, 'I want nothing to do with you . . . right now.'

Slim Redden let his hand go back to rub his nose. Redden said, 'No fight here, boss.'

Bassett showed that cynical smile again, and again it rubbed against Jack Farrell. Bassett said, 'Just forget your farmers, Farrell, and we'll get along. Cut them off the vine and let them die. When they leave we'll turn their cabins into linecamps and rip up their fences.'

Jack was silent.

Bassett looked at him again. Redden had turned and was moving toward the front door, and his smile was one of victory as he looked at Mrs. Stebbins. But the woman's face was blank under his gaze.

Bassett turned, too.

Jack thought, I shouldn't do this, but he knew he would. He came in noiselessly behind Bassett. His left boot went out, going ahead of the man. Jack pushed against the broad back.

Bassett lurched ahead. He grunted something, but Jack's slamming hand against his back garbled the words. Bassett tripped over Jack's boot. They went down and Jack was on top, sitting on Bassett.

Mrs. Stebbins had the shotgun out, the barrel on Slim Redden. Redden had stopped and whirled, a slender, quick-moving cat. Mrs. Stebbins cocked the shotgun.

'Just stay where you are, and put your hands up!'

By this time, Jack had jerked Ross Bassett's pearl-handled gun from its holster. He threw it to one side, the Colt skidding along the floor to wham into a counter and stop.

Jack stood up.

'Even up now, Bassett,' the storekeeper growled.

# CHAPTER FOUR

Bassett got to his boots, wiping dust from his shirt. He sent a hot glance at Slim Redden and anger ran across him as he saw his range-boss standing under Mrs. Stebbins' shotgun.

Jack said, 'He's out of the play. There's a twelve gauge cartridge in that shotgun, primed with number five shot. At that short range it would blast a hole in a man that a fellow could put his doubled fist into.'

He kept watching Bassett, and he saw the man recover his sanity. Bassett looked at his gun and said, 'You still pack hardware, Farrell.'

Jack tossed his gun into his office. It landed on the couch standing along the far wall. It made a little *plunk*.

Jack said, 'Fists, fellow, fists.'

Bassett hit at him. It was a short left hook. It was vicious. It had the kick of a mule. It traveled just a few inches. It was meant to be a surprise blow. But it wasn't.

Jack stepped inside of it, circling to the right. The left hook slid past him. He stepped in and shot a left and right into Bassett's low ribs. He heard the man grunt, caught his wince. The blows had hurt.

But he couldn't fight Bassett at close range.

Only a fool would go in and mix with the man at arm's length. Bassett outweighed him by quite a few pounds. Bassett was stockier and had more strength.

Something smashed into Jack's jaw. He found himself with his back to his office. Bassett looked unreal and weird, coming toward him. The man was crouched, and he looked like an ape moving ahead with his paws up.

Jack moved to the left, sliding along the wall. Bassett penned him in, hitting. Behind Bassett came the muffled sounds of a man giving encouragement. That would be Slim Redden cheering on his boss.

Jack thought, If Redden finds out that shotgun is empty he'll break into this. This can't last long. He fought up and ahead, breaking away from the wall. His arms were tired and blood made a salt taste against his tongue. He drove Bassett back, fighting hard.

They were wrecking the Merc. Already a stand that had held bolts of cloth was on its side, the bolts on the floor. But that thought held no place. The main point was to whip Ross Bassett.

This was more than a mere fist-fight. Other things were at stake beside winning this brutal, mauling fight. Jack Farrell, fighting as hard as he could, was aware of that.

The loser of this fight would also lose prestige here in Wild River Basin. If Ross

Bassett whipped him, then Bassett's domination would be increased; the farmers would really be afraid of him. A victory for Bassett would also be a victory for the other Wild River cowman, old Milo Dawson. Word would go out, 'Ross Bassett beat up on Jack Farrell. Hades, us farmers ain't got much of a chance now, what with that cowman whippin' our leader.'

But if he whipped Bassett, then the boot would be on the other foot. Bassett would lose some of the danger he personified to the farmers. He, Jack Farrell, would be a real leader, a tough gent who could handle himself in a tight spot. Jack knew this; he gave the fight all he had.

He had been in many fights before. Every cow-country kid had to get into fights in school or in town. He had whipped his share of his opponents. A few of them had fought to a draw with him. A few had whipped him. But this was the toughest fight he had ever been in.

For one thing, the previous fights had been trivial in importance: a fight over a name called in anger, or over a horse-race, or over some minor thing. But the fate of his leadership here in Wild River Basin depended on his winning this fight. This fight had great importance.

And he knew, with a sudden burst of his second wind, that he was winning. For now he had Ross Bassett moving back. Bassett's blows had lost their sharpness and had acquired a tired, mauling desperation. Bassett was gasping for air, grabbing for fresh strength that did not seem to arrive.

Redden hollered, 'Nail him, Ross! Get 'im down an' feed 'im the boots. Tackle him, Ross!'

The words were dim and distant, beating through the fight. But evidently Bassett heeded them. He bunched and made a tackle, his gross body moving ahead. Jack just had strength and agility enough to move to one side. And as Bassett came in, Jack him hit.

The blow was looping and it had lots of luck. For it smashed against Bassett's jaw, high on the right side, under the cowman's ear. Jack thought, That got him, and he moved back, for Bassett lay on his belly.

Bassett moved his arms back, braced himself, and slowly rolled over. He tried to get up, got to one knee, then bent his head down. He had a cut under his right eye and on his upper lip.

Jack stood, legs braced wide, having eyes only for Bassett. For if the man got up—Suddenly he turned, warned by Mrs. Stebbins' cry.

'Jack!'

He tried to duck. The object was big, whistling through the air. It came at express-train speed. He knew it was a heavy iron skillet and he knew Slim Redden had flung it.

It whammed into his head and he went down. When he regained his sight he was sitting on the floor, back to the wall of his office, and Mrs. Stebbins and Martha were kneeling beside him. Somebody pounded on the front door.

'Got a customer,' Jack said. 'Let him in.'

Martha said, 'That door stays closed, Jack! Jack, you look a sight, man. Oh, why, oh, why do you fool men have to fight?'

Sanity returned to Jack. He looked around. Slim Redden and Ross Bassett were gone. Martha and Mrs. Stebbins and he were the Merc's only inhabitants. He looked at his clerk.

'I must've been out for a while, Nellie.'

'Not long.'

Mrs. Stebbins got to her feet, apron over her face. Her sobs hurt Jack as much as the stinging left by Ross Bassett's fists.

'I—I pulled the trigger, Jack. The gun—it just clicked; it had no loads. He threw a skillet at you!'

She kept on crying. Martha had a cloth and some water and she kept washing Jack's face. The lovely blond girl was very serious, her sweet face dark with her thoughts; but she kept silent.

Mrs. Stebbins walked to the front of the store. She found a chair and put her head on a counter and sobbed. Jack knew she was not crying because of the fight. It was a thing long past, even though only a few minutes old.

Nellie Stebbins was crying because of the trouble ahead. Jack knew, with grim reality, that the woman was right. This fist-fight had settled nothing. He had not whipped Ross Bassett convincingly. The heavy iron skillet, flung by Slim Redden, had seen to that.

Nor had Bassett whipped him, either.

Therefore they stood on almost the same ground they had occupied previous to the fist-fight. Each had tasted the other's fists, though; now each knew the other's physical strength. And Jack doubted if Ross Bassett wanted any more fist-fighting. Bassett would settle this in his own way now.

Jack knew what that way would be: with a gun. Mrs. Stebbins knew it, too; therefore the woman had broken down and wept. And this knowledge, bitter in its intensity, was also written on Martha's face.

Jack asked, 'Am I cut bad?'

'Not too bad,' Martha said. 'On your jaw, Jack; your right eye might get black. Your lips are puffed.'

'How'd he look?'

Slim Redden had taken his boss to the doctor's office. She had seen and known instantly what was wrong, and she had hurried to the Mercantile.

'I didn't look carefully at him, Jack. His

face—it was all blood. I came running, and Mrs. Stebbins was hysterical. No, don't get up—sit down, please.'

'I have to get up.'

His knees were not too strong, but they held him. There was a wildness in him, a driving unrest, which matched his physical strength. They collided, and the wildness and unrest died before the weakness and sickness left from the fight.

Jack got into his office, where he had to sit down. He put his head in his hands and bent forward and tried not to think.

Finally Martha said, 'Here comes the doctor.'

Mrs. Stebbins let the medico in, then relocked the door. The doctor was an old man, fat and puffing, who had arrived some twenty years before to visit the Dawson Rafter T Ranch during a vacation, and to get in some hunting and cow-punching. He had never left Wild River Basin. He acted as a veterinary and a medical doctor both. He wasn't the best doctor in the world, but he was a blessing to Wild River Basin.

'You danged fool, Jack. Don't you know that fists never solved nothing? I thought old Martin Farrell had taught you that.'

'You come to lecture me or to heal me?'

'Don't get loose-tongued with me, you young whippersnapper.' The medico knelt beside him. He gave Jack's wounds a brief

53

inspection. 'Ross Bassett can't see out of one eye. His jaw don't track right. You hit him on the jaw with a hammer or a mallet?'

'My right.'

The medico stood and opened his bag. 'Lie back in the chair with the back of your head across the back-piece. Martha, unscrew that iodine, please.'

Jack winced.

The storekeeper winced even harder when the iodine grabbed hold. He gritted his teeth and tears came to his eyes. Martha took his hand. The girl's grip was reassuring but it did not compensate for the sting of the iodine.

'You danged horse-doctor—'

'Sit still!'

Jack gripped Martha's hand, concentrating on that effort to try to forget the bite of the medicament. Finally the doctor recorked the bottle and put it in his bag. He looked at Jack, smiling slightly.

'You aren't as bad as Bassett, at that. I guess, if a winner had to be picked, you'd be he, Jack.'

'Compliment?'

'A word to a damned fool.' The medico gruffly snapped shut his bag. 'This fight didn't end anything, and don't josh yourself about that.'

The medico walked through the wreckage, tipped his hat to Mrs. Stebbins, and the clerk left her chair to let him out. But she kept the

54

door locked. She went to work picking up the bolts of cloth and brushing the dust from them.

'Have to have a rummage sale.' Jack hoped it was a joke.

'That isn't funny, Jack.'

Jack looked up at Martha. The iodine had taken the sting out of his bruises. He must have looked like a pinto with the iodine marking him.

'I must look like a paint bronc.'

'That has no humor, either.'

Jack said, 'I had to fight, Martha. He called me. They came here to kill me. This range is busting open with trouble.'

'Where will it end?'

Jack said, 'Where else can it end?'

She knew full well what he meant. The trouble had run its course, and now guns would finish it. It had gone beyond the rim of enmity, beyond the interference of the law—if there had been a lawman in Wild City.

This registered on her pretty face, laying over its loveliness a look of utter despair that touched Jack Farrell, making him understand then how much she loved him. Without this girl on this grass, this land and his hopes, he realized, meant nothing. The thought had been with him for a long, long time. But before, it had never moved in the revealing spotlight of clarity.

This trouble, climaxed by his fight with Bassett, had matured this emotion. Light had revealed it in all its dazzling power. Up to the present each had acknowledged the love of the other and had accepted it. But it had lacked depth and structure, and now stress had added these two elements.

Jack said, 'Honey, don't look like that. It-it hurts me . . .'

She went to her knees and put her head on his arm. He couldn't see her face now, but he knew the despair that was there. He could feel it, and the thought was large and uncomfortable.

'Martha—'

She said, 'Dad's in this, too. He's old and stubborn and cattle are his way. Mother has talked to him. I've talked to him. His back is made of whang-leather, and it's only stubbornness.'

Jack waited.

'Mother and I—we've talked and talked. Cows, they're done here: he knows it, but he won't admit it. We've told him the farmers could raise cattle—better cattle—because of grain and feed.'

'What did he say?'

'What could he say? Nothing. We've told him to buy hay from farmers, to cut hay—Last winter showed him a lot. I believe he intends to put up wild hay.'

'That's good.'

She looked up, and he saw her slow tears. 'I don't want to cry. But a woman has to cry when a man cannot, Jack. Dad might change—we'll make him change!—but Ross Bassett is made of a mold. Bassett won't change!'

She was weeping silently. Her head was on his hand on the arm of his chair. He felt her tears. Her shoulders shook a little. And he moved his other hand—a skinned, swollen hand—and put it on her back.

He opened his mouth, intending to say, 'Martha,' but he knew the words were of no use. He did not say them. He sat there, feeling her sobs, and he looked straight ahead.

And he felt a thousand years old . . .


## CHAPTER FIVE

The pinto pawed the dust in nervousness. He wanted the trail and he wanted the smell of sage. But the bridle-reins held him and he rolled the cricket in his bit to show his displeasure.

Martha Dawson said, 'Mr. Bassett.'

Ross Bassett and Slim Redden had just come from the Ace Up. Bassett turned and said, 'Miss Martha,' and his swollen lips showed what was supposed to be a smile. But

Jack Farrell's fists had broken the smile for some days.

Bassett came up and put his hand on the pinto's mane. Martha said, 'When you ride for home I want to ride with you and talk to you.'

'And about what, pretty maiden?' There was a touch of gallantry in this man. But she saw it did not wear well for it was too superficial.

'I want to talk to you.'

Bassett turned to Redden. 'Slim, ride that South Fork bog country. I'll meet you at the ranch.'

Slim Redden said, 'You're the boss, Ross,' and looked and smiled at Martha Dawson. He was being given the run-around and he knew it. 'You never ask to ride with me, Miss Martha.'

'Some other time,' Martha said.

Slim Redden moved toward his horse tied to the hitch-rail, walking in the stooped, deadly manner that was habitual with him. He found stirrup and went up and gave the Mercantile a long, slow look. Martha got the impression that the look was so hard it would go through the walls to pick out Jack Farrell. Then Redden neckreined his sorrel and loped away with dust idle behind him.

Bassett found saddle. 'Let's ride, Martha.'

They let their horses lope for a mile, with the pinto a head in front of Bassett's bay.

Martha glanced at the man and saw his solidness in the saddle. He was solid all the way: on foot and in saddle. This was characteristic of him, and she wondered if in his strength Ross Bassett did not have his greatest weakness.

Bassett said, 'Hot day to run a bronc,' and reined to a walk.

Martha kept silent, letting her pinto find his pace. She had decided to let him break the silence and bring up the question. He knew what she wanted to talk about, she was sure. And he would be figuring she would be the one to bring up the subject. She decided to play herself against his curiosity.

The sun was hot, bringing lather to their broncs. The pinto's headstall and the edges of the Navajo saddle blanket soon were rimmed with foam. A few Northern Yuccas were in bloom, and their flowers were waxen and dainty on rocky foothills. Sage was strong, sending out its pungent aroma; ahead, a sagehen and her small chickens moved across the trail, disappearing into the sagebrush and greasewood.

They went three miles and at last Bassett said, 'All right, you win. Now what did you want to talk about?'

Her arm made a circling gesture. 'This basin, Ross.'

His face showed a sourness that training swept aside. He leaned against his near

59

stirrup and thereby turned his bulk against his saddle. And when he spoke his voice was not much more than a strong whisper.

'It's no use, Miss Martha. I appreciate your interest, but it's no use. Better we leave our words unsaid.'

Again she got that weird feeling of futility. He was steel inside, and wild horses could not pull him. She matched her own purpose against this steel and made her voice almost light.

'Ross, there's room for all of us. You and Dad can run cattle back in the hills. You can feed summers in the mountains.'

'Where would we feed winters?' He answered himself. 'We can't run winter-pasture in the valley any longer. Look what happened last winter. I lost thousands of cows against the nesters' fences.'

She waited, preparing arguments.

He went on with, 'Had those fences not been there, Martha, I would never had much winter-kill. But my cows wandered up to them in blizzards. They piled up and died on the prairie when fences kept them from brush.'

'Buy hay from the farmers.'

He spread skinned, bearish hands. 'Sure, that might be an out. Then cattle would cost too much to raise. That would mean extra money, and the market can't stand it. It would break my Triangle S.'

She pointed out, 'Cattle are low now, that's true. But the market is bound to go up.' She played her last card. 'Ross, you know where this will end, don't you?' She gave him no time to answer. 'There'll be a street or a strip of night and range, and you and Jack Farrell will be shooting across it.'

She was calm now. The breakdown back there in the Merc had steeled her and drawn all emotion from her.

Ross Bassett shrugged, was silent.

They rode on for a mile and then they came to the fork. They pulled in and Bassett said, 'Let me tell you my side. I never met my father; my mother died before I could remember. Texas cattle and Texas trails took me. I looked for land—free land—and I found it on Wild River.'

He was steel again. A knife—or a bullet—couldn't dull that steel. She got that impression, and it was strange and uncomfortable.

'You've had a home. Therefore it might be impossible for you to understand what goes on and drives a man who's had nothing and has fought for every bit of food, every stitch on his back. I've built my Triangle S. Now they're trying to drag it down.'

'You have to make a compromise with progress.'

'Do you call these farmers progress? I don't. I think they'll set this country back if they get their footholds. I can make a compromise with a worthwhile thing, but not with these farmers.'

'Then my words are useless?'

'Useless.'

She played with her rope-strap. She looked down and noticed her hands trembled. He saw this too.

'You love Jack Farrell?'

'Yes.'

'You're afraid for him?'

'I am, Ross.'

He looked at the distant cone of Mount Baldy. He seemed interested in that bleak upthrust of rock. 'I feel sorry, in a way, Miss Martha. For you, because I admire you, and if I could ever love a woman, it would be a woman somewhat like you, only older and more grown-up. But I can't love a woman. I can't love a horse or a dog. Why is that?'

'Greed?'

'No, not greed.' He shrugged, put his eyes back on her, folded his hands over his saddlehorn. 'I guess I wasn't made for emotion. Maybe back there—' his right hand made a gesture '—I lost something. Could that be it?'

'God help you, Ross Bassett.'

'God won't help me, Martha. Only one man ever helped Ross Bassett, and that was himself. Where does your father stand?'

'As stubborn as you do and in the same

spot.'

'That's good.'

She said, 'We'll change him. He's an old fool. Mother and I will change his mind.'

He looked at her and he did not smile. 'I believe you,' he said at length. 'I believe, Miss Martha, that if you made up your mind you could stop the sun.' He was stiff again, unyielding.

She left him there, and that old futility was inside her. She was feminine and lovely and still she had not changed him. Her personality had met his, and hers had bounded back as though it had collided with stone. This was not pleasant. It gave her a vague sense of inferiority.

She remembered him sitting his pony at the fork and watching her ride towards the Rafter T. He had sat there with his hands folded across the wide horn of his Texas saddle and watched her. His eyes had been almost a physical force casting its impact against her. And she knew, had she been able to see those eyes, that they would have been unreadable. They were a mystery.

She turned her horse over to the old hostler to unsaddle and feed. By this time the feeling of inferiority had somewhat departed. But never did the raw pressure of the danger covering this grass leave her. Not for a second would it go. For the core of it swirled around Jack Farrell.

The house was long and rambling, almost covered with wild morning-glories. She came into the dim, cool living room with its rock fireplace and its smell of tobacco-smoke and the coolness of thick walls.

'Martha.'

Her mother sat in her wheel-chair in the doorway leading to the hall. Martha said 'Howdy, Mom,' and kissed her. 'I got the thread.'

Her mother wheeled into the room, hands firm on the wheels. She said, 'El Malone was in town. He came out with the news of the fight.' Her eyes were sharp as auger-points.

This information sort of upset her plans. She had hoped to keep the news from her mother until she had talked with her father. But that was out of the question now.

'How did El come to be in town?'

'Broke his catch-rope pulling a cow out of the bog, he said, and he rode to town for another. He heard about Ross Bassett jumping that farmer Stanton, too.' Ada Dawson sent shrewd eyes probing her daughter. 'Was Jack hurt bad?'

She told her the extent of Jack's injuries.

'Why don't you marry him, Martha?'

'He hasn't asked me yet.'

Ada Dawson made clucking sounds. 'A young man has to be led, young lady. But I doubt if he'd marry you, anyway.' She hurriedly continued, 'Not until this trouble is

64

settled, anyway.'

'He's right,' Martha said.

Her mother nodded. 'Of course he's right. Everybody knows that but Ross Bassett and a few bone-headed ignorant cowboys. Even some of the cowboys know their day is done, but Bassett pays top wages and they're fools enough to want to die for money.'

'And Dad, too.'

Again a vigorous nod. 'Yes, and your father has a stiff back, too. He must have swallowed a poker.' Shrewd eyes peered out the window. 'There he rides into the barn now. I guess by this time he's heard about the fight. Word got around through the farmers right fast, El reported. And word has probably got to your father.'

Martha nodded.

Her mother asked, 'What's your plan, child?'

Martha told about her talk with Ross Bassett. 'I can't change him a bit. Neither can I talk any sense into Jack.'

'Jack can't back out. Neither can Bassett. Bassett's pride won't let him. Jack's got his entire future tied up here. He has to stay. Only thing that can bring about a peaceful settlement is that Bassett and Jack work together.'

'That can't be done . . . it seems.'

Ada Dawson said, 'Cheer up, child. You can be sure your father is pulling out of this

65

mess, and we might just as well have the showdown right now.'

Martha crossed the room and put her hand on her mother's thin hand. 'Both of us together, Mommy.'

They waited until Milo Dawson came across the porch, spur rowels clanging. He was saddle-tough and saddle-wise, this old cowman; he knew the ways of horses and men . . . and women. And when he stopped and looked at them this accumulated knowledge, gained by day after day of living, shone in his sunken eyes.

'My two women, huh? How are you?'

Martha said, 'All right.'

Instantly Milo Dawson was on guard. He held his hat in his right hand, looking at them. Finally he asked, 'Should I turn and stampede out the door, chicken?'

Ada Dawson said, 'Come over here, Dad.'

He knew what was going on. This information showed in his face, and Martha wondered, with a sudden sickening feeling, just how their conference would turn out. She could only use her wits . . . and hope.

'I'll take it standing here,' Milo Dawson said.

Martha asked, 'You've heard about the fight, I suppose? And how Ross Bassett jumped on Max Stanton?'

'I have.'

Martha looked at him. He was showing his

age and looking old—in fact, he was old. Soon he'd be under the ground. That thought was not new to her. She had long dallied with it and fortified herself against that time. The thing that struck her odd was that, regardless of how old a man is, he'll frequently fight for something material to the point of giving his life, and sometimes beyond that point. And, in view of the few days he had left, the whole thing was a waste of time, effort, and breath. She had told that to Ross Bassett.

Ada Dawson drummed on the wheel of her wheel-chair. Martha said, 'Mr. Stanton has his elderly mother living with him. She's the only kin he has, he told me last week.'

'What does that mean in this?' Milo Dawson spoke roughly.

Martha knew the roughness, as far as it concerned her and her mother, was just a pose to cover up her father's real nature.

Ada Dawson said, 'Don't talk so stupid, Dad.'

Martha told her about her talk with Ross Bassett and his unyielding position. Milo Dawson listened, watching her. He knew this gave no enjoyment either to his wife or daughter.

'You've got two ways to turn,' Martha said. 'One is to hook up with Bassett and go against these grangers with fire and lead. The other is to surrender to Time and work with the farmers.'

'That sounds easy, girl. Right nice and easy, the way you say it. That's because you've never fought to raise cattle, to run an iron—you never fought flood, prairie-fire, Injuns, and blizzards.'

'Those things are not concerned in this,' Ada Dawson said sharply.

Martha said, 'I don't want to see you dead, Dad.'

For a moment, emotions tugged at Milo Dawson's weather-beaten, gaunt face. Pain showed in his time-dulled eyes that even now were watering a little from the wind and sun. He looked at his wife and then slowly lifted his gaze to his daughter.

'I haven't got many days left, at best.'

'But a bullet won't end them,' Ada Dawson snapped. 'We'll see to that. Either you work with these farmers—raise hay and cut it and put in dams and irrigate—or Martha and I are leaving.'

Martha started to say something, stopped. Her mother was playing their trump card. And when she said something, she meant it.

Milo Dawson said, 'Give me a few days to think it over?'

In the end, they consented.

# CHAPTER SIX

Ross Bassett sat his saddle, hands laced across the wide horn. Bassett sat there and watched her ride toward the Rafter T and he thought, Maybe she's right. Maybe because she's a woman she sees things a man cannot see.

Then he smiled at this. A smile that formed slowly, for his lips were not fitted for a smile; Jack Farrell's fists had seen to that. And the memory of the fight in the Mercantile brought his thoughts momentarily to Jack Farrell. But not for long, for they swung back to Martha Dawson.

He thought, She loves Farrell.

But what place had that thought? None that he could find. There was no niche in which to store it. Martha Dawson loved Jack Farrell and millions of women and millions of men—yes, billions and trillions of them—had loved in time before. Martha Dawson meant nothing to him.

She had tried to make him over. She had advanced logical arguments and she had done a good job in expressing them.

A woman was that way, he decided. They always wanted to change a man. They wanted him to bend his character to theirs, and the battle was endless. And in the same way a man tried to make a woman conform to his viewpoint.

But that philosophy—if it could be called by that name—had no place here. By this time, Martha Dawson was out of sight. She had rounded the hill, and the toe of the rocky butte had reached out to hide her. Still he sat there, hands across the horn—his skinned, swollen hands.

He looked at the mountains, finding in them some comfort. They were cold and aloof and they were like him: nothing stirred them, either. He wondered if he had not unconsciously shaped his personality after the mountains. For each morning, upon coming out of the Triangle S ranch-house, he looked up at those mountains.

But still, they were not the same in character. He wanted grass and cattle and he wanted to boss men. The mountains were alien and neutral. Always neutral, they stood against the storms, against the moon, and they had no plans.

He remembered Martha Dawson's warm beauty. This was sharp and fleeting, yet it had quick effect. By all rights that beauty should have stirred him. But it hadn't, though it stirred other men.

He turned his horse.

He rode fast, ruthlessness pushing him. Under his saddle the muscles moved and pulled apart, part of an endless pattern long familiar through experience. He whipped

Martha Dawson from his mind.

Slim Redden came out of the brush that footed Black Butte. Redden said, 'Waitin' for you,' and Ross Bassett pulled his bronc in. Redden said, 'I rode those bogs. No cattle in them. It was a way to keep me from riding and spoiling your talk with Martha.'

Something in the gunman's tone jerked Bassett's gaze towards him. 'You too, Slim?' the Triangle S man asked.

'Me, too,' Slim assured him.

Ross Bassett laughed soundlessly. 'She makes men come to her,' he said. 'She has no eyes for you. She's only got eyes for Farrell. You oughta know that by now. Farrell's piggin'-string has her tied.'

Slim laughed, and his laugh made a sound. They swung broncs, put home hooks, and Bassett took the lead, ponies running against the day. They were wild, and this took hold of them, and they ran with wild abandon. This went to their broncs and the animals responded, stretching and running across the prairie—brown spots against the great panorama of brownness. Slim laughed and moved his bronc up ahead and they rounded the bend and the Triangle S lay ahead of them.

A stone house, built in the form of a U, sat back against a naked black butte, cast of dark igneous rock. The butte shadowed the house in summer, bringing coolness; when winter came, it broke the savage thrust of the blizzard.

They went down in front of the stone barn, scattering chickens and ducks. A guinea-hen had started shouting on first seeing them and was still making a wild clatter from the roof of the blacksmith shop.

'Mozo!'

The young Sioux buck came running from the barn. He grabbed reins and Bassett's bronc reared, forefeet slashing. The young Indian jerked him down and swore at him. Bassett grinned.

'Talk tough to him, War Bonnet.'

Slim Redden looked at the cook-shack and its smoke. Men were going into the bunkhouse. They had finished their day chores and would wash and loaf for a while before supper.

'He's hollerin' inside of me,' Redden said. 'He wants chuck.'

'Feed him and then come to the house.'

Redden looked inquiringly at him and asked, 'A night ride, maybe?'

'Maybe.'

Redden moved away, still dissatisfied. Ross Bassett went to the house. He walked across the rock and concrete floor of the living room with its tanned pelts and homemade rawhide and willow furniture. He stuck his head in a door and yelled, 'Here he comes, Willow Girl.'

72

'I hear you.'

The squaw worked at her big range. By this time the kitchen was cool and he went close, hearing the frying of spuds and steak. Coffee bubbled in the pot. He said, 'My horse tried to front-foot your boy.'

Dark eyes turned on him. 'Horse hurt him?'

'Not War Bonnet.' Bassett chuckled and lifted the lid of the frying pan. 'That looks good.' For a moment his eyes showed something; then convention drew a satin screen across them. 'I'll wait in the living room.'

'That's all right.'

He went into the living room, got a newspaper from the stand, and tried to read it. For one thing, the room was rather dark; for another, the paper held no interest even though it was the county paper and he knew lots of names mentioned in it. He threw it to one side.

The time had come to act, to break open and drive this to a conclusion. Up to now there had been little action. They had squared off and looked for weak spots and done little destruction. Of course they had cut the Doyle ditch—but wasn't Bob Pasco building a dam on Beaver Creek?

He thought of this dam.

He spread across his mind a map of the Wild River country. He knew every gully and

73

creek, and the map was plain. He picked out spots on it and contemplated them. But his mind kept returning to the dam Pasco was building.

'Supper ready, Mr. Bassett.'

He ate alone. Out in the kitchen he could hear the squaw talking to her boy as they ate. Willow Girl was a good cook. She had worked for him many years, keeping a tidy house and cooking good meals. The squaw's husband had been killed in the Custer Massacre when her boy had been a baby. She had left the Sioux teepees and gone to work for him.

He ate slowly. Outside the sunlight died, blended into twilight; the twilight stayed, folding the raw crevices of the earth. The wind died down with the sun, then lashed up again within an hour. It sang in the eaves. Its song took up a higher rhythm as the velocity increased.

Willow Girl lit the lamp, stopped and looked at him. 'I hear about fight,' she finally said.

He nodded, then was silent.

She looked at him for some time. Then she turned and went back to the kitchen. She and War Bonnet talked in Sioux. He understood a few words, but most of the conversation was alien to him. War Bonnet went down the hall to his room and his mother worked on the dishes. This completed, he heard her also go to her room. Except for the wind, the big

74

rock house was silent.

He read the paper, the kerosene lamp sending dancing shadows across the darkness, moving the shadows across the floor and furniture. At ten o'clock, Slim Redden came in.

'Poker game,' Redden said. 'Same old poker games.'

Ross Bassett put the newspaper on the table. He leaned back in his chair, feeling the urge to go to bed and sleep. He opened his eyes.

'Ready, Slim?'

Redden shrugged. 'You lead the way.'

Bassett listened to the wind. Outside, it talked and danced and jibbered. The rock walls turned it. Here it was warm and a bed was good . . . For the last time he shoved that thought into the discard.

'Win any money?'

Redden swore with a cold deliberateness. 'You tryin' to string me, Bassett? Man, did you ever see me win a poker game?'

Ross Bassett pulled on a buckskin jacket, his back to Redden so the trail-boss would not see the smile of the Triangle S owner. This was an old joke between them, but it never failed to get a rise out of Slim Redden. Bassett buckled on his gun, fitting the holster on his thigh.

'That old girl down there—that Mrs. Stebbins—she didn't want me to pick up your

Colt back there in the Merc. I never figgered at any time she'd let the hammer fall on that scattergun, an' I was danged lucky the thing was empty.'

'More than lucky.'

Redden stood beside the door. 'Where do we go, boss?'

Ross Bassett went out on the porch, the wind whipping his jacket. 'Doyle,' he said. 'Mike Doyle.'

'Cut another ditch?'

'Cut a fence.'

Redden said, 'We need fence-pliers, then. My rifle's on my saddle. I guess yours is still in holster, too.' He was checking, running over this thing that was to come, building toward it. Then he followed Ross Bassett, who was moving through the night. The wind whipped up dust.

Redden tasted the dust and found it unpleasant. He spat with the wind. Then they were in the barn. A lighted lantern hung from a stall-partition and the horses showed wide eyes in its light.

'Dark horse,' Bassett said.

Redden said, 'I've got that much brains.' He was irritable and his voice showed this, and Bassett smiled in the darkness. Saddles lifted, came down; cinches slipped as latigoes tightened.

Redden said, 'I'll get some wire-cutters.'

Redden moved into the night and Bassett

led their broncs outside, standing in the shelter of the two black geldings. Redden came back and said, 'Here's a pair for you,' and Bassett tied the fence-pliers to his back saddle-strings.

Redden said, 'Anything else?'

'Not that I know of. Not much of a chore.'

Redden put his bronc close and the wind took away his chuckle. 'Sometimes they run big. I mind one time down on the Cimarron. Wire-cutters' war, it was. Looked peaceful, a wide stretch of wire, but they started to talk, those guns did. Since then everything looks big to this saddle-monkey.'

Ross Bassett put his bronc to a lope. They angled across Wild River Basin; they crossed the river at Rocky Ford. Steel-shod hoofs rasped against rock and spray shot up. There in the boxelders, sheltered from the wind, Bassett laid his hand on Redden's reins.

'How goes it?' Redden wanted to know.

Bassett said quietly, 'No cigarets, savvy? Nothing to give away our position in the dark. This is Milo Dawson's range. But you know that and there's no need me telling you that.'

'Go on.'

'Dawson's got cattle along the Doyle fences. They want that alfalfa. They want to get into that grain, too. No grass hardly on open range.'

'That's it.'

'We cut that fence in about a dozen places, one riding each side. Then Dawson cattle go in, and by morning that alfalfa and wheat will look sick. Dawson'll get the blame.'

'Which side do I ride?'

'Take your choice.'

Redden said, 'I ride the east side.'

Bassett looked at the Montana sky. 'No moon. Wind to cover up sound. All right, Redden, all right.'

Then Bassett rode off alone. Redden swung east, for the farm was about a mile ahead. And as he rode, the trail-boss loosened his fence-pliers. He saw cattle, and because they were on this side of Wild River, they were Dawson Rafter T cattle. Ross Bassett was right. Rafter T cattle were gaunt and they wanted green feed, and they were deviling Doyle's fence to get at the greenery inside. Once that fence was cut, Rafter T cattle would stream in.

The wind lifted Redden's hat, and he tightened his jaw-strap. He rode through the cattle and moved them aside and they scampered like big rabbits in the night. Redden found himself thinking, Wonder if the Doyles have a guard out? Maybe somebody would ride the fence.

He came to a slight depression and sat his bronc in it, a screen of bullberry bushes ahead of him. With darkness across the range, it was harder to judge his position; he

78

found landmarks, knew then his exact location. A cow bawled and then a calf answered, and these were the only sounds outside of the wind. Redden rode forward, and came from the coulee into the fence.

His horse almost ran into it. Redden put him parallel to the fence, leaned down; his wire-cutters made three fine clicks. Wires parted; tension left the fence. Redden looked into the night, something stirring in him. He sat there a moment and then rode on, and about ten rods further he cut the fence again. Behind him cattle were moving into the breach.

This was too easy.

He was making his fifth cut when a voice said, 'Who rides there?' There was a ditch beyond the fence, and the man spoke from there. Redden came up in saddle, and his fence-pliers found his belt. His hand left them and came back to his gun.

'Who rides?'

Redden thought, 'Sonny Doyle,' and he raised his .45. He knew that any moment a bullet might tear into him, and he wanted to be first. That was screaming in him, and his .45 lifted in hot challenge.

He got a glimpse of a form on the dike, and he shot again. The youth was about sixty feet away, and Redden pulled back his hammer. His bronc reared, throwing his gun high; he held the hammer, pulled the gun down.

Something hit him in the belly.

He made a fine, high whine. He felt something pluck at his belly. He knew, at that moment, that a rifle bullet had hit him. A steel-jacketed rifle bullet that had not mushroomed. For the blow had not been a slugging one; it had been quick and hard and clean.

It doubled him.

He heard another bullet whine, the sound unreal and close. By this time his bronc had turned of its own accord and bolted. He found himself low over his horn, reins down on the fork, one hand gripping the horn. He didn't remember leaving the fence, for pain had gutted him. But he did remember levelling his six-shooter and running it dry against the gun that had shot him.

No more bullets came. And that seemed odd. For by rights Sonny Doyle would have emptied his rifle against him. The irony of the thing was plain, biting with the dig of the bullet; a raid had turned wrong, and a teen-age kid had turned it. He holstered his empty .45.

The bronc rushed through cattle, scattering them. He had free rein and he was frightened and he ran toward the river. Redden straightened, sucking in air, and then he caught control of himself and his horse.

Ross Bassett rode up. 'What went wrong?'

'The kid. Sonny Doyle.' Redden was

80

panting, sick and weak. 'He ambushed me. Behind that dike.'

'Where?'

'Belly. Lord, I'm sick. I'm—Ross, what the hell does a man feel like when he's goin' to die?'

'I don't know. What a question to ask! I've never died yet!' Momentary anger ran across Ross Bassett. And that anger was not directed toward the blundering of Slim Redden. Rather its impact was aimed against the unruly fickleness of Lady Luck who had turned tables on them.

'Can you ride?'

'I gotta ride.'

Bassett said, 'Follow me; we got to get out of here.' They loped on, and Bassett hollered, 'Did you get the button?'

'I dunno.'

Bassett said, 'She sure bit us, huh?'

There was no answer to that. Within twenty minutes, by hard riding, they had reached Wild River and crossed it. Bassett said, 'We'll make Post Hole line-camp, Slim. About a mile. Can you make it?'

'I'll try.'

Bassett rode beside his man now, reaching out occasionally to hold him in saddle. Redden was low, and he kept putting down a hand to hold it against the neck scarf he had pushed against his belly. His shirt was open and the tails flapped in the wind.

Redden said, 'Just a punk kid, and I've lifted guns against good men. Just a kid, with the night and luck on his side—'

Bassett said, 'That was enough.'

Redden swore with husky anger. 'I'll run him down, Ross. I'll show him the way of a gun! I'll get him in town and—'

Bassett caught him. They were in front of the single roomed log line-camp. Bassett said, 'They can't trail us here. Those farmers ain't no hands at trailin'.'

'I'll kill him,' Redden repeated. 'I can walk, Ross. You open the door.'

Bassett swung the door open. Redden took a step, then another—he folded and Bassett caught him. Bassett carried him inside and, because of long occupancy in this cabin, he found the bunk in the dark.

He got Redden on it and Redden lay back, sighing. Bassett found the lamp and lighted it and placed it on the handmade table. Then he came back to Slim Redden. He stood there and looked at him.

He stood there for some time.

Outside a bronc stomped, angry at the wind. The wind bent cottonwoods and boxelders and made them creak in protest. But Ross Bassett did not hear the sounds.

The lamplight was bright. It filled the small room, bounded off the rough logs, found reflection in the tinware on the stove. It limned the shaggy head of Ross Bassett.

Finally Bassett reached down.

His forefinger found the spot on Slim Redden's throat. It held there, pushing against the side of the windpipe. The hand moved over and took Redden's wrist. Redden's hand lopped over, fingers bent.

Bassett pulled back his hand. He wiped it unconsciously on his chaps. The line was thin. No man knew when he would cross it. That thought was controlled and orderly and calm. You came to this line and you walked along its edge, just as Slim Redden had ridden parallel to that fence. Then something material broke and you crossed the line and that was all.

Bassett said, 'Sorry, Slim, sorry.'

Three words. The lamplight took them and put them against the wall and they died. Bassett turned and went outside. He went to the lean-to barn and lit a match. A broken latigo strap hung on a hook. He took it back into the house.

Sitting crosslegged on the floor, he cut the strap into four strong strips. He tied a strip to each of Redden's wrists, one to each ankle. He thought, I wish I had some wire. Water might affect that latigo leather.

He considered that angle.

He said, 'I'll bury him instead.'

He went outside and found a shovel and he tied this to his saddle. He unsaddled Redden's black, peeled the bridle from the beast, and turned him loose. He went back and blew out the lamp and carried Redden outside. The man was a sack of meal, broken in the middle and sagging.

His horse shied and Bassett jerked him around and found his saddle, with Slim Redden forked across the back of the kak. Bassett rode toward the foothills, one hand back of him to hold Redden.

An hour later they came to the right cut-coulee.

Bassett said, 'This is it,' and went down. He got Redden and laid him on the soil. False dawn was here, giving a faint light. Bassett found the spot, looked at it and judged it.

He went back to Redden and carried him under the lip of the cut-coulee. He laid the man on his back and covered his face with his shirt, leaving the wound bare. Then he climbed up ten feet and reached the top of the cut.

He poked with his shovel, looking for a weak spot. He found it and got his shovel into it. He pushed on the handle, then pulled back.

The soil was stubborn. The handle sagged, gave, held. Bassett closed his eyes, bootheels braced; he pulled. He felt the sod give. He pulled harder and was rewarded when the handle suddenly sprang back.

He scrambled up the slope. Earth slid down—dried, loose earth. It settled around the man known as Slim Redden. The last Bassett saw of his trail-boss was when the dust slid across Redden's bare chest.

Bassett worked a while longer with the shovel, putting down more dirt. Sweat formed across his shoulders and his tongue got heavy. He worked about an hour, and by this time dawn was with him.

Finally he rode for the Triangle S.


# CHAPTER SEVEN

Nellie Stebbins pulled her robe around her. 'Doc woke me up,' she said. 'He wanted me to help him. But I came over to tell you first, Jack.'

'Thanks.'

'He isn't shot bad,' the woman said. 'Doc says the bullet didn't come out, though.'

'I'll be right over to Doc's office.'

Mrs. Stebbins left and Jack swung out of bed, feet cold on the floor. Hurriedly he dressed. He started out of his bedroom, then went back and got his gunbelt and .45.

Outside he met Bob Pasco. The farmer said, 'I came in last night late and stayed in town overnight at the hotel. The hullabaloo woke me up. Reckon somebody shot Sonny Doyle, I hear?'

'Mrs. Stebbins just told me, Bob. I don't

know anything about it.'

When they reached Doc's office they pushed past the few people standing around outside. Pasco said, 'They get up early when there's some excitement.' Jack nodded, and they entered the waiting-room.

'Who's out there?' came Doc's voice from the side room.

'Jack and Bob Pasco.'

'Don't let anybody else in. This isn't no racetrack.'

Jack slid the bolt on the door. Bob Pasco removed his hat and sat down, plainly uncomfortable. Mrs. Doyle came from the side room, crying. She sat on the divan and hid her face in a big handkerchief.

Mrs. Stebbins came in, wearing a white apron. 'Don't carry on like that, Mrs. Doyle. He isn't hurt very bad.'

'They'll kill us all,' the farmer's wife sobbed.

Mrs. Stebbins looked at Jack and shook her head before she went back into the side room. Mrs. Doyle kept on crying. In about five minutes, Mike Doyle came out of the side room.

Jack looked at the farmer. 'Can you tell us what happened, Mike?'

Doyle said, 'The kid was riding the fence. Somebody cut it. Instead of coming after me, he crept up the irrigation ditch and started to shoot it out. He got one through the right shoulder.'

'Rifle bullet?'

'Doc says it was a pistol ca'tridge.'

Jack said, 'I'm danged sorry.' What else was there for him to say?

Mrs. Doyle looked up, her eyes red. 'You should be sorry, Mr. Farrell.' Her voice dripped acid. 'You got us unsuspecting, peaceful country folks out here, and it looks like we'll all get killed!'

'Close your mouth!' Doyle ordered roughly.

The woman returned to her handkerchief. Bob Pasco glanced at Jack and got up and went outside with Mike Doyle bolting the door against him. Jack felt pretty low. He could stand up against a woman but a woman and her sharp tongue were a different proposition.

He looked back at Doyle. 'What time did it happen?'

Doyle told him.

Jack asked, 'Did Sonny recognize the man who shot him?'

'Too dark,' Doyle said.

Jack stood up. 'Wonder if he shot the gent?'

Doyle looked at his wife. 'No,' he said. Jack went into the side room, and the farmer followed. He grabbed Jack's sleeve. 'I didn't want the missus to hear, Jack. Sonny says he's sure he hit the gent. The man was on horseback. Sonny said he bent over and rode away like blazes.'

'Then we look for a wounded man,' Jack said.

Doc met Jack at the door. The medico said, 'We're putting him under ether . . . I'll have to dig for that bullet. Lodged in under his shoulder blade. I've had worse jobs.'

'What can I do, Doc?'

'Get Mrs. Doyle out of here.'

Jack Farrell looked at Mike Doyle. 'That'll be your job, Mike. She don't cotton much to me. Take her to the hotel and have the clerk send the bill over to me.'

Doyle said, 'I got some money.'

Doyle left and Jack heard the farmer talking in a low tone to his wife. Mrs. Stebbins was taking Sonny's pulse. The boy slept peacefully, his face pale. Jack looked at his shoulder.

'Game kid,' Jack said.

The doc said, 'A bullet doesn't give a damn who it kills.'

The outer door opened and closed. Doyle was taking his wife to the hotel. Jack said, 'Nothing I can do here.' Mrs. Stebbins followed him to the door. 'Jack, don't do anything rash, please!'

Jack asked, 'What would it be, Nellie?' His smile was not happy. 'Nobody seems to know who jumped Sonny. One thing is certain it's either Dawson and his men, or Ross Bassett and his Triangle S punchers.'

'Play your cards close.'

'I sure will, Nellie.'

Outside, the town blacksmith got Jack aside. 'We should get the militia in, Jack. This is turning into a range war.'

Jack said sourly, 'I wrote to the governor. So far I've had no reply. I don't expect one either. The governor and Bassett and Dawson are all common. They stick together like fleas on the same dog.'

Jack went toward home. Bob Pasco came out of an alley. Pasco said, 'I've got two men guarding my reservoir. On guard all the time. Where you going, Jack?'

'Out to that fence.'

Pasco's face was strained in the dawn. Finally he said, 'I'll ride along. We might find something. That kid got in some shots. He might have connected. I'll meet you on the edge of town. My bronc is in the hotel barn.'

Pasco moved away, big in the uncertain light.

Jack saddled his bronc, the pony nuzzling his sleeve. Things had piled up fast, circumstance running against circumstance, and he didn't feel too spry. He kept remembering Mrs. Doyle's angry words.

The farmer's wife was upset; perhaps had she been normal she would not have snapped at him like that. She was only in the same mood and frame of mind as were many of the other wives. Jack figured the women were his biggest enemies here on Wild River range.

He knew, for sure, that a number of the farm-women were continuously harping on their husbands, getting them to leave Wild River Basin. They were in mortal fear for themselves and their children and husbands. And the shooting of Sonny Doyle would only increase that apprehension.

He had feared a happening similar to this. For a moment dismay had his way with him. Maybe he should abandon his whole scheme? Maybe he should let Wild River Basin remain the property of cattle?

But he knew, even as these thoughts plagued him, that he would not give up as long as a farmer remained on this grass. Even with his limited resources he was ready to purchase the land of any farmer who made up his mind to abandon his homestead.

Jack realized he could purchase this land on jawbone. If a farmer did leave, he would take a few dollars cash for his spread, instead of going out empty-handed, abandoning his property and hard work to either Milo Dawson or Ross Bassett. With Jack paying between twenty-five cents an acre, the farmer would have a hundred dollars or so to a section of land.

But he did not want this to happen. In unity and numbers lay strength; he needed each and every farmer. Mike Doyle could speak for himself—he would stay despite his wife's entreaties. Mike Doyle's boy had been shot and Mike was Irish enough not to run, but to stay and fight.

He needed more men like Mike Doyle.

He met Bob Pasco, and Pasco said, 'We'll ride out to the spot where the shootin' happened, huh?'

Jack Farrell nodded.

By this time the dawn was clear. Pasco said, 'You don't seem none too happy, Jack.'

'Can you blame me?'

Pasco looked at his pony's ears. 'Mrs. Doyle'll carry on some. She's quite a power among the women-folks, too, I'd say.' His smile was rueful. 'Seems like the women that can talk the fastest and mostest and say the least is the leader all the time.'

Jack said, 'Us men are just as bad.'

Pasco's broad face showed a quick smile. 'By hades, I sure can't please you, Jack. Yeah, it done nobody no good. Some of these farmers got purty shaky boots right now, I'll betcha. And some of their wives got their tongues sharpened to a danged fine point.'

Every word the farmer said was true. They grated against Jack Farrell, were all the more powerful because of the helplessness of Jack's position. This was like getting into a fist-fight in the dark with pillows tied to your fists. You didn't know where to hit or whom you were fighting, and if you did manage to hit your opponent you did not hurt him.

'Who do you figure did it, Bob?'

Pasco rubbed his whiskery jaw. 'One of two men did it or had it ordered, Jack. Dawson or Bassett.'

'Great help,' Jack said sourly.

'I'd say Dawson.'

Jack looked at him sharply. 'Why Milo Dawson more than Ross Bassett?'

Bob Pasco explained. Didn't Milo Dawson run cattle on this side of Wild River? And weren't Milo Dawson's cattle skin-poor from the lack of grass due to the drouth? And wasn't Mike Doyle settled smack on range claimed by Dawson through squatter's rights?

'Way it looks to me is this, Jack: Dawson's either cut the fence or had some of his men cut it. Then his stock could get into Doyle's pasture and fields and clean out that oats and grain in one night. Them cows are hungry. They'd tie into that head-grain and mow it down by morning.'

Jack saw logic in the farmer's summation. Too darned much logic. He could only nod confirmation. He didn't dare open his mouth to defend Milo Dawson. If he had, Pasco would think he were defending the cowman because of Martha.

And in his logic, the farmer was right. The cutting of Doyle's fence would benefit Milo Dawson more than it would help Ross Bassett. Of course the act—and the resultant gun fight—could scare nesters from Bassett's range, too. But to the casual observer, it would appear that Dawson stood to benefit the more.

'Maybe some day we'll know,' was all Jack could say.

But he doubted the premise that old Milo Dawson had cut the fence, or that Dawson or one of his men had exchanged shots with young Sonny. He had known Dawson all his life: the cowman did not seem one to fight in the dark. But still, a man could never tell. Dawson was old and had his back to the wall. Despite the assurances of Martha that her father would not fight, Jack was not too sure about the old cowman's stand in this farmer-cowman war.

And war it was, he decided. He had tried to keep open warfare down because of the effect on his farmers. But he had failed in that.

He'd failed in lots of things lately.

They loped down the wagon-road, a jackrabbit running ahead. Suddenly the rabbit bounded into the brush. Prairie chickens rose and settled in the brush ahead. Trails of lazy smoke marked the blue of the basin as the farmers prepared breakfast and got ready for the long day ahead.

A neighbor's son—a youth of about nineteen—guarded the Doyle home. He came out of the barn, carrying a Winchester.

'Was up in the haymow. Good place to look

down on the outfit. How's Sonny?'

'He'll pull through,' Jack assured. 'We're lookin' aroun', Jake.'

'Hop to it.'

The boy went back into the barn, and Jack and Bob Pasco rode across the pasture. Some of Dawson's Rafter T cattle were in the alfalfa, and the grain crops were pretty well eaten down. Jack cursed silently. The loss of that wheat would hit Doyle hard. Of course he could salvage some wheat; about one half the crop was gone though, or so Jack figured.

They hazed the Rafter T stock ahead of them, putting the cattle out through a cut in the barbwire fence. Pasco had picked up a fence-pliers and a length of barbwire at the Doyle farm, and they dismounted and looked for tracks. Cattle hoofs and cattle manure marked the soil. Also, the wind had blown hard, and had swept the dust away down to the hardpan soil.

'Can't see no trace here,' Pasco said.

They patched the fence, and rode to the next cut. Here they picked up the tracks of a shod horse. They repaired another cut and rode down the fence to where the irrigation ditch swung out to run parallel with the fence.

'Here's Sonny's tracks,' Pasco said. 'Here's where he's laid down and shot, and there's some of his blood.'

Jack was walking along the cut spot in the

94

fence. He said, 'Come here, Bob,' and Pasco slid down the ditch, the loose earth rolling ahead of him. Jack was kneeling, and Pasco knelt beside him.

'Blood,' Pasco said.

Jack put his finger on the spot. The blood was dry, and he rubbed it idly into the dust. He got to his feet and walked back and forth, searching the ground. 'No more blood, but it looks like this rider headed north, Pasco.'

Bob Pasco said, 'Rider coming, Jack.'

## CHAPTER EIGHT

They sat their broncs and looked at the Dawson puncher. The man asked, 'How did them Rafter T cows get into Doyle's fields?'

Jack answered: 'Somebody cut Doyle's fences last night.'

'Good idea.'

Jack looked at Bob Pasco. Then he looked back at the Dawson Rafter T cowboy. He didn't know this rider very well. He heard the man's name was Rodtem. Rodtem had hired out to the Rafter T during spring roundup. He had drifted in, and Milo Dawson had needed hands.

Pasco said, 'Maybe a Dawson hand cut this fence, huh?'

For the first time, it seemed as if Rodtem

understood the full significance of this situation. Jack Farrell saw the cowboy's face darken, saw the ugly gleam light his yellow eyes.

'Might have been,' Rodtem admitted.

Jack said, 'No trouble, men.'

But Pasco was adamant. 'If I ever catch you or any other man—be he either from the Rafter T or Bassett's Triangle S—ridin' my fence I'll call him, Rodtem. And you can bet your last bottom buck on that, too!'

Rodtem showed a cynical smile. 'You talk tough, punkin roller.'

Jack Farrell saw there was trouble ahead. He knew the limits of husky Bob Pasco's temper. Rodtem was armed, packing a short-gun in a worn holster, and Jack figured the cowpuncher knew how to use that gun. He looked like the gunslinger type. There had been a time when no man packed a short-gun on this range. Men had packed Winchesters in saddle-boots, but they had been used against coyotes and wolves that could cut into the calf crop.

But now every rider packed a gun. Even some of the Wild City citizens, he had noticed, went armed.

Bob Pasco was armed, but Jack knew the man was slow with his weapon. And he had a hunch Rodtem was just egging Pasco on into trouble. So Jack put his horse ahead, driving him between the broncs of Pasco and the

Rafter T man.

Pasco said, 'Hold on, Farrell! This is my deal!' Pasco reached for the bridle on Jack's horse, aiming to move the bronc back.

Jack said, 'Don't, Pasco.'

Pasco pulled his hand back, looked at Jack. Rodtem had his right hand down on the fork of his saddle; the left held his reins. He looked at Jack and his lips showed their cynicism.

'Shieldin' your sodbusters, huh, Farrell?'

Jack knew that Rodtem expected him to go for his gun. But he did not draw; instead, he hit. A smashing straight-out blow that caught Rodtem on the jaw. Jack heard the surprise in the cowpuncher's wheezing grunt.

Rodtem reached for his gun. But he was stunned, and Jack beat him to the weapon, for the butt was close to him. Sunlight twinkled on steel as the gun slid out to plow to a stop in the dust.

Rodtem growled a curse, and hit at Jack. But Jack's other blow came in and Rodtem left his saddle. Quick as a roper getting down to hogtie a steer, Jack Farrell left his hull, hit spike-heels into the dust. He moved around Rodtem's bronc, fists up. Rodtem was getting to his feet.

'You got a gun,' Rodtem raged. 'I'm disarmed.'

Jack handed his pistol to Bob Pasco. 'Keep that for me, huh?' And as he did so, Rodtem kicked him. The man's boot broke hard against Jack's groin, making pain shoot through him.

The kick doubled Jack. He almost went down. Rodtem came in, hitting now; he missed his first blow, connected with the second. Jack Farrell went back and sat down, almost out.

'No boots!' Pasco hollered.

But rage controlled the Rafter T cowpuncher. Even though Bob Pasco was the only man armed, Rodtem went ahead. He kicked and the blow hit Jack in the shoulder. Jack rolled, and Rodtem's second kick missed.

Hurriedly, Bob Pasco was dismounting. Then the farmer stopped suddenly. For Rodtem was down. It had happened like a flash. Rodtem had kicked again. Jack Farrell had caught the man's upraised leg, jerked down hard. And he had thrown Rodtem.

Pasco encouraged, 'Get up, Jack!'

But his advise was wasted, for Jack was already on his feet. By this time, the dull haze had left him; his mind was almost clear. He had rage but, unlike Rodtem, he held it. He knew that rage had no place in a fist-fight. Fist-fights were won by cool logic, not distorted anger.

Rodtem scrambled up, as yet unhurt. Jack's side was burning with fire. He walked into Rodtem. They were about the same size, but Jack knew more about fighting. Rodtem came in, they met, they broke. And Rodtem was the one to give.

A few minutes later, Rodtem lay on the ground and Jack stood wide-legged, weary arms holding up skinned fists, looking down at the Dawson rider.

'You—you got enough?' Jack panted.

Rodtem blew blood from his nose. 'I got enough.' Jack watched the man get slowly to his feet, and this time the merchant was braced against a kick or sudden tackle.

Rodtem, though, had spoken the truth. He wiped his face on his sleeve and went to his bronc. He said, 'You can handle your dukes, Farrell. But maybe you ain't so handy with a gun.'

Jack said, 'I have nothing against you. I don't want to kill you. We have no reason to go for our weapons.'

'I think we have.'

Jack looked up at Bob Pasco, who had mounted again. Pasco read the sickness and loathing in the merchant's eyes.

Pasco said, 'You've got my gun to account for too, Rodtem.'

Rodtem said, looking at the farmer, 'You're just a sodman—an ignorant farmer—and you don't amount to much.'

Anger flushed Pasco's face.

Jack said, 'Take it easy, Bob.'

Pasco settled back, his eyes clear now. Jack

got Rodtem's gun and unloaded it. He took the cartridges from the man's belt, tossing them into the dirt. He got the cowboy's Winchester off the saddle, and broke it and ejected the shells.

Rodtem said, 'You take no chances.' He was cynical again and scoffing.

Jack nodded. 'Not with a rattlesnake of a killer like you, fellow. Why a man like Milo Dawson would hire such a gunman is beyond me. You're not back-shootin' us from the brush unless you ride to the ranch or to town for cartridges. I know your kind.'

Rodtem's lip peeled back.

Jack continued. 'There was a time—and not so long ago—that we'd tar and feather a man like you and run you out of the country. But those days seem to have gone for a while.'

'We'll get them back,' Pasco promised.

Rodtem climbed up, turned his horse. He said, 'There'll be another time,' and loped away. He headed for Smith's ford on Beaver Creek, which was on the way to the Rafter T ranch-house.

'He'll have a story to tell old Milo,' Pasco reminded him.

Jack said, 'The devil with him and with Milo Dawson, too. If he's that danged ignorant, the old fool, he should hit for the Hot Place.' His good nature returned. 'Bet my face sure looks pretty, huh, Bob? Right

100

after having that fist set-to with Ross Bassett, too.'

'You'd win no purty contest.'

Jack said slowly, 'Maybe I shouldn't have fought him. But it looked like he aimed to jump you, and I thought of your woman and kids, 'cause you both had your hands close to your guns.'

'Thanks, Jack.'

They watched until the foothills hid Rodtem. Then they set to work seeking sign pointing toward the direction the night-rider had taken. They followed the trail to the end of Doyle's fence, and here another rider came in. Pasco found some blood here.

'Right trail, Jack.'

But they lost the pair of hoofs when they reached the wagon-road. They paused there and gave this matter speculation. Had the pair ridden toward Wild City or headed toward the Ford?

Jack said, 'I asked Doc if a wounded man—outside of Sonny—had come to him. He said no. I was wondering if Sonny had connected.'

'If that man's stung bad, sooner or later Doc'll be called to treat him,' Pasco reminded him.

Jack said, 'We'll ride toward the Ford. You watch that side and I'll watch this. That way we can tell if two riders break off this trail.'

They rode toward Wild River. Jack felt of

his jaw, wiggled it; he saw Pasco's grin. He smiled. 'Still got a jawbone in it,' he said. 'I came out pretty lucky.'

'Rodtem didn't.'

When they came to the buckbrush and timber flanking Wild River, they drew rein again. The dank smell of the water came to them, and the sound of rifles, running across the rocks, made a whispering, gurgling sound.

Pasco said, 'Ol' Tim Montrose has some catfish lines set along the bank here. The bobber is under on every line, see. He's got a big catch this mornin'.'

'Good eating.'

Pasco said, 'Another rider comin'.'

Jack had seen the pinto across the stream moving through the brush along the road. But now he acted as if he had not noticed the horse and rider before. 'Looks like Martha Dawson's cayuse.'

They waited until the golden-haired girl was sitting her horse in front of them. And again the beauty of her stirred Jack Farrell, stirring to life in him a dull happiness. But in this happiness was a haunting sickness. Between them stood this trouble: a high wall neither had as yet broken down.

'I saw Rodtem yonder, Jack. He just rode past without talking, but it looked like a horse had kicked him.'

Jack doubled his fist suggestively.

Martha looked from Jack to Bob Pasco.

Jack noticed that the farmer did not meet her slow gaze. He understood why. She was Milo Dawson's daughter and Pasco was a sodman. By accident of birth and work they were not friends. Now he realized, in its full significance, why some of the farmers did not trust him. He and Martha were in love.

That was a mark against him. There was a rumor around that one farmer openly claimed Jack was working in cahoots with old Milo Dawson. His assumptions were logical, too, and therefore all the more destructive.

'What did you fight about?'

Jack told her the entire story. He told about Sonny Doyle being shot, how Sonny was in the doc's office in Wild City, how he and Bob Pasco had patched the Doyle fences after driving out Dawson Rafter T cattle from Doyle's grain- and alfalfa-fields.

He noticed Pasco watched the girl carefully. Jack too kept his gaze on her tanned, sweet face. Pasco was watching to see what effect—if any—Jack's words would have on the daughter of old Milo Dawson, owner of the big Rafter T. The Rafter T, one of the two spreads that were fighting the farmers.

But Jack thought her face registered only surprise. He was sure of that. Then logic came in to whisper, If old Milo Dawson did cut that fence—or order it cut—he'd not have told his daughter about it. Therefore Martha could register nothing but surprise.

Bob Pasco asked, 'And you didn't know about this until Jack told you?'

The implication was clear. She was Milo Dawson's daughter. Dawson's cattle had gone through a cut fence to eat down Doyle's crops.

'No, Mr. Pasco, I did not know!'

Pasco looked at Jack. Pasco shrugged. The farmer said, 'We'd best get on, Jack, and see what we can find.'

Jack wondered why Martha was riding range this early in the morning. It turned out she was looking for some of her saddle-horses. The mozo had forgotten and had not locked the night-pasture gate. One of the horses had worked with it, rubbing the lift-latch with his nose, and had managed to open the gate.

'Saw two sorrels and a gray over yonder,' Jack said. 'Them looked like your saddle-horses. I wondered why they were out on the range.'

Martha rode away. Bob Pasco took his eyes from her and looked at Jack. 'She didn't like what I said, I reckon.'

'You're suspicious. You have a right to be. She's a cowman's daughter.'

Pasco spoke very slowly. 'Maybe you don't know about it, Jack, and if you don't, I don't want the news to hurt you. I'm your friend. You're my friend. But some of the farmers are against you because of Martha.'

Anger touched Jack Farrell. 'They're stupid,' he growled. 'I've heard that talk. Some even claim I aim to sell their homesteads out to Milo Dawson after they leave. I see where their talk is logical, too, and that's the danged part that hurts. I ought to get mad, but I can't; it's too far-fetched.'

Pasco seemed talking to himself. 'The day of open range is done. Dawson knows it. He has to run cattle on land he owns. Yes, they're saying that—you'll get their homesteads if they leave, buying them for a few bucks. Then they claim you'll turn around and peddle to Dawson and Dawson will have the patented range he needs and has to have.'

'Hogwash, Bob!'

'I know it is. But lots of these farmers think different.'

They followed the trail to the edge of the ford. No riders had branched off; they'd crossed Wild River.

Jack said, 'Looks like Ross Bassett's work. His range is on the other side of the river, and these riders must've crossed.'

Pasco nodded. 'Might be. Still, it would be a trick played by Dawson, too. A fox doesn't run his tracks direct to his den. He travels over to Mr. Coyote's den, taking any possible pursuers to him. Then he doubles back to his own den.'

'Could be.'

They crossed Wild River and stopped on the far side to let their broncs drink. Then they rode out onto range claimed by Ross Bassett.

## CHAPTER NINE

The black horse grazed in a clearing. Here there was some grass, for the buckbrush had held lots of snow and this had soaked into the ground and put in a good sub-moisture.

Jack said, 'You stay here,' and while Pasco sat bronc in the brush, the merchant rode around the black horse. Evidently the bronc had been recently ridden and he was hungry. He did not bolt, but he stood and looked at Jack, then resumed grazing. Jack rode back to Pasco.

'What iron on him, Farrell?'

'Triangle S.'

Pasco murmured, 'One of Bassett's broncs, huh? Long ways from the home ranch he is. Sweat marks on him and marks of a saddle-blanket. Dang it, that bronc looks danged familiar to me.'

'You sure you don't know him?'

Pasco looked at him. 'Ain't that the black geldin' that Slim Redden rides?'

Jack nodded, 'That's him, all right. A light blaze in his face, and the off-front foot with a stocking.'

Pasco growled, 'Sure, it's him, all right. We're wastin' our time. He's done strayed and wasn't curried good before he was let loose. That's how come he packs them sweat marks yet.'

Jack had to admit the farmer was right. Horses had a way of straying—especially saddle-stock that wanted to get as far away from man as possible to keep from being ridden. The wildest of the wild horses had once been broken either to saddle or harness. They knew all the indignities man could force them into. That's why they went with the wild bunch and were the wildest of the wild.

Pasco asked, 'What'll we do?'

'Keep riding, I'd say.'

They went out of the brush. Here two broncs had left the trail. They dismounted and searched for blood but found none. Nor could they track the ponies long, for the tracks ran into the lava ledges that came down to flank Wild River. And lava did not carry marks, not even of a shod hoof.

'We're runnin' at this wild,' Pasco grumbled.

Again Jack had to admit the farmer was correct. He put his premise bluntly. 'Pasco, you and me cut that fence, savvy? I got a slug in me. You came in from cuttin' the other side of the fence. You took me across Wild River. That sign points toward Ross Bassett

107

and a hand.'

Pasco rubbed his whiskers, scowling widely. 'Keep on.'

'I'm sick, danged sick. What would you do first?'

Pasco scowled again. 'I'd head in for some shelter. I'd look your wound over and see what I could do for you before we rode too far.'

'Where would you go?'

Pasco looked around, eyes probing the brush, the hills, the prairie beyond. 'Any shacks around here a man could hole up in?'

Jack Farrell braced himself against his saddle's fork. He rocked back and forth. 'You said something, friend. You'd head for a camp. One close by, too. Up on Post Hole Crick.'

'How far?'

'About two miles. Right where Post Hole enters Wild River.' Jack waved his forearm. 'Over that way.'

'Tracks lead that way,' Pasco said.

Jack took the lead, Pasco loping behind. They broke through rosebushes, thorns catching their chaps, sliding off the thick leather. Jack thought, Maybe this is a wild goose chase. Maybe Pasco is right: mebbe Dawson was behind it and he was the fox and he threw out this cold trail.

That was the trouble with this whole thing. It was all guesswork. Hit or miss, and mostly miss. Nothing concrete against either Milo Dawson or Ross Bassett. Just guesswork, nothing more. Guesswork . . .

He thought of Sonny Doyle, back in town. Sonny Doyle, with a bullet hole in his shoulder: red-haired, grinning Sonny. He liked the kid. But the kid had a lot to learn. He was too cocky, too make-believe tough. Maybe this shooting spell, and the bullet—well, it might have shown Sonny he wasn't so tough.

He liked Sonny, sure. But he liked lots of kids: Billy Stebbins, Mack Ellison, Joe Fogarty. He wasn't doing this only because of Sonny. Nor was he doing it only for himself, as some farmers had suspected and even hinted.

That was the thing that hurt. When people started to distrust you it hurt you. And it hurt more when you were doing your best work. And this work was directed, really, toward the farmers. Of course, there was no evasion of facts. With farmers in Wild River Basin—farmers with money to spend—his store would prosper.

But hadn't he himself taken up a quarter-section, filed also on a hill claim, then a desert claim? He controlled a section of this land. And he had made improvements—he'd run a fence, broken a quarter-section to the plow. Yet some of his farmers distrusted him.

Jack finally surrendered to the inevitable

and let his thoughts die. His fight with Rodtem ought to show the doubting farmers his side was with them, not with Milo Dawson. He had whipped a Dawson man.

He said, 'Pasco, we'll have to get the farmers at a meeting. Some of them need to be kicked in the pants and given some backbone.'

Pasco nodded. 'When and where?'

'Tomorrow night. At the church.'

'Good idea. We'll get word around, Jack.'

They skirted a jutting butte that ran toward Wild River. Then came more brush and a winding trail; finally Post Hole Creek was ahead. They crossed it and rode toward the Triangle S cabin that stood in the clearing.

'Hello the house.'

No answer. Jack called again; still no answer. He and Bob Pasco dismounted, soil-tied their broncs with dragging reins, and went into the cabin. Line-camps were never locked. Many a cowpuncher had saved his life during a blizzard by seeking shelter in a line-camp. The unwritten law of the range said a line-camp should never be locked. Each man using it should keep it as clean as when he came. This latter was the only requirement.

The interior was musty. The floor was clean and Jack looked at it first, and what he saw made his breath come faster.

Pasco breathed, 'Blood, huh?'

Jack stood silent, looking at the single room. A cast-iron stove and crooked stove-pipe, a few handmade chairs and a handmade table, a shelf beyond the stove that held cans of pepper and salt and a few canned beans—all this he saw and to all this he paid no attention. For the bunk held his attention.

The bedding was ruffled. But there was nothing odd in that—evidently the last man who had used the cabin had not made the bed. The significant thing was that spots of blood showed on the tough blanket.

'More blood,' Pasco said.

Jack summed it up. 'Somebody's taken the wounded man here. This is on Ross Bassett range. But that, of course, proves nothing, as we've figured before. Anyway, one thing is certain.'

Pasco listened, rubbing his whiskers.

'A raider stopped one of Sonny's slugs. Our job is to keep our eyes open and try to find out who that nightrider was. We know he's either on the payroll of Milo Dawson or Ross Bassett.'

'Let's ride over and talk to Dawson, huh?'

Jack scowled. 'That ain't a bad idea. We got another chance to check, too. If this wounded gent ain't dead, he should show up sooner or later at Doc's office for treatment down in town.'

'Doc'd not tell, though.'

Jack nodded. 'I know that. But we could

111

get somebody to watch his office. Billy Stebbins would do it.'

They went outside, and the latch slid into place behind them. They looked for tracks, found none; Bob Pasco looked at the wild run of Wild River. Jack Farrell knew what thoughts bothered the farmer.

'If that gent died and if somebody tossed him in there, we'd probably never find his body,' Jack had to admit.

Pasco jerked himself around. They mounted and rode toward the Dawson Rafter T. When they arrived at the ranch, Martha was just corralling her errant saddle-horses. Her pinto was flecked with sweat from his run.

'Your dad around, Martha?'

She turned clear blue eyes on Jack and regarded him steadily. 'What do you want to see him about?'

Jack said, 'We came in peace.'

The blue eyes found Bob Pasco and studied him. 'He's in his office, Jack. You know where it is—that log building this side of the bunkhouse.'

'I know where it is.'

Martha sat on the top rail of the corral, watching them ride past the blacksmith shop where two cowboys and the smithy were shoeing a bronc. A guinea-hen had started her raucous racket when they had been a quarter-mile from the ranch. Perched on the

112

stable, she continued her noise.

Pasco said, 'They didn't have a guard out.'

'The guinea-hen,' Jack explained.

Pasco didn't understand, and his eyes showed his question. Jack went on to say that a guinea-hen was the best watchdog a ranch could have. 'If a hen could be classed as a watchdog,' he said, smiling a little. 'It started back in the days when the Crows and Siouxs used to raid ranches. Guinea-hens could pick up their advance, even when a dog failed.'

'Ross Bassett has them too,' Pasco said.

Jack nodded at the smithy and the cowpunchers, who were watching them. He spoke quietly. 'Unless I'm wrong, Milo Dawson has had a guard out, too. He's not showed himself from the brush. See that gent going out the back door of the office? He's rid in ahead of us to warn Milo we were coming.'

'Smart move.'

They dismounted and Milo Dawson called, 'Come in.' The office was small but well-furnished with Indian rugs, a buffalo-hide on the couch, and Milo Dawson sat behind his big desk, working on some paper.

Dawson said to Bob Pasco, 'Never figured I'd see one of you farmers ride peaceful into my ranch.'

Pasco said, almost gruffly, 'You saw it Mr. Dawson.'

Milo Dawson caught the edge of the

113

farmer's surliness, and looked at Jack Farrell. 'Martha told me about the trouble at the Doyle farm, Jack.'

Jack's gaze met that of Bob Pasco. Milo Dawson had got the jump on them. Jack told about the blood-spots they had found and trailed to the Post Hole Creek linecamp.

'Milo, we'll lay our cards on the table. You know and I know and Pasco knows that either your outfit or the Bassett Triangle S cut that fence and shot that kid. If you did it, you've got a wounded man on your premises—unless you've taken him into Doc while we were out trailing.'

Dawson's face was the color of muddy water. 'Are you accusing me, Jack, of fallin' so low I'd stage a midnight fence-raid against a danged farmer?'

Pasco cut in. 'Your cattle ate down Mike Doyle's head-grain. They profited by cutting that fence, Dawson. Your cattle almost ate down Doyle's crop and that means no money for Doyle this harvest!'

Dawson's tongue came out, wet his lips; his teeth clicked. 'You done speakin', *hoeman?*'

Anger flushed Pasco's dark face. 'No, I'm not, *cowman!* We're not askin' for trouble, us farmers ain't; but if you want to shoot dirty pool, we'll shoot that kind of pool, too. How about your man, Rodtem?'

'What about him?'

Jack said, 'Not so fast, Pasco.' The

merchant realized he'd have to get the play away from the farmer. Pasco had too much temper. Jack spoke to Milo Dawson. 'Rodtem was riding toward Doyle's fence. He jumped Pasco, and I moved in and knocked your man from his bronc. We fought and I hope I trimmed him. What was he doing over by that cut fence?'

The door opened behind them. Martha came in, was silent, put her back against the wall, listened. They took their eyes back from her.

Dawson showed a little smile. He was standing now, hands into fists, knuckles on the desk holding his weight. He said crisply, 'So that's what worries you two wild buckos, huh? Well, it got me worried, too.'

Again Jack Farrell and Bob Pasco exchanged glances.

Jack asked, 'We don't follow you.'

Dawson said, 'Rodtem came to me. Told me about that fight, figuring I'd send men out to help him get you two out on open range. I tied into him and canned him. I'm as much at sea about him being over by that fence as you are.'

'You ran him off the ranch?' Jack asked.

Martha said, 'He did, Jack.'

Dawson said, 'Girl, I can handle this.' Suddenly he was old. He was bent under a silent weight. He looked at his gnarled, rope-calloused hands, eyes hidden from Jack and Pasco. The silence grew, and Martha's gaze met Jack's. Her blue eyes were very old, very worldly.

Pasco said slowly, 'By heaven, I believe you, Milo Dawson. I've doubted it up to now, but now I don't figure you hate us farmers. Do you give me your word that neither you or your men cut that fence and shot that kid?'

'My word, sir.'

Pasco said, 'I'm sorry I doubted you, sir.'

Dawson looked at the farmer. 'I moved into this basin when the Sioux held it, Mr. Pasco. I killed off buffalo to have grass for my cattle. The Cheyennes burned down my first ranch-house. Mrs. Dawson and my daughter and myself hid in the cellar. I've had riders go out, and when we found them they'd have skulls split open and the reds had lifted their scalps.'

Pasco nodded. Jack listened. Martha's mouth was open a little. An old cowman was talking about a life that had been, a life that the westward march of an empire had broken into a million glistening pieces.

'I've fought blizzard, drouth, man and beast. I've fought them all with force. But this is the first time I've been defeated. And, by God, it wasn't force that defeated me, either: it was time.

Pasco said, 'We're holding a farmers'

meetin' tomorrow night at the church, Mister Dawson.'

'I'll be there.'

## CHAPTER TEN

Ross Bassett held a cold branding-iron and looked at Jack Farrell, who still sat his saddle. 'What the hades you doin' here, you farmer-lover?'

Jack glanced at two of Bassett's hands. They were untying a colt they had just branded. The colt scrambled to his feet, the newly made Triangle S iron on his left shoulder. The hands stood there, looking at him. Jack took his gaze back to Ross Bassett.

'There's a hand of yours standing in the barn door,' Jack said quietly. 'He's got a rifle on me. I don't like to have a Winchester covering me, Bassett.'

'You don't, huh?' Cynically.

Jack waved his hand back at the hills behind him. 'Up in that brush I got five farmers staked out,' he lied. 'They've got rifles on us right now.'

'My guard said you came in alone.'

Jack said, 'I rode in alone, sure. But I stationed them farmers out there before I rode in, and your guard didn't see them. He ain't got very good eyes or ears, Bassett. You should set out a better man for a guard.'

117

Ross Bassett walked across the corral and stuck the branding-iron in the small fire made of cowchips. 'Just stick around,' he told his two hands. 'We'll brand these colts later.' He came back to where Jack sat his bronc, and looked at the hills covered with brush.

'I don't think you've got guards out there, Farrell.'

Jack shrugged. 'Your privilege, Bassett. I didn't come for trouble. I just want to know if you've got a wounded man on your hands.'

'Wounded man?'

Jack thought, He sounds sincere and surprised. But he knew Bassett was a good hand at concealing his emotions. Past experience—some bitter—had taught that to him.

'Sonny Doyle shot the man who plugged him,' Jack went on. He kept one eye on the man in the barn with the rifle. 'Pasco and me trailed him to your Hole Crick line-camp. Blood on the bed there. Redden's bronc was in the brush, and he showed sweat-marks.'

'I don't follow you. I heard about Doyle having a run-in with night-riders, but I figured it was old Milo Dawson that was hitting him. He's settled smack-dab in Milo's range.'

'Where's Redden?'

Bassett looked at one of his riders. 'Where's Slim Redden?'

'Riding the north line of hills, I think.' The

man shrugged. 'Seems to me somebody told me he pulled out early 'cause them cattle over there might drift too far back into the rough country.'

Bassett swung his narrow eyes back to Jack Farrell. 'There's your answer, scissorbill. You can bet your last bottom buck that none of us jumped the Doyles. 'Cause when the Triangle S jumps into action, it won't be a little thing like cuttin' some stupid hoeman's fence, and you can lay money on that.'

Jack said, 'Could I search the premises?'

'What for?'

'I'd like to see if you've got a wounded man here.'

Bassett said, 'Search and be damned. Go ahead.' He walked over to his branding-irons. 'Rope another colt, Windy.' He seemed to ignore Jack Farrell completely. Windy laid his loop on a colt, catching him by the front feet. The colt hit the end of the rope and went down. The other puncher jumped on him, tied him by three feet.

'Hot iron, Ross.'

Bassett pulled an iron out of the fire and ran across the corral. Jack caught the wry odor of burning hair and horsehide. The colt neighed in pain; the process took but a few seconds.

While the punchers untied the colt, Bassett carried the branding-iron back to the fire, arranged it so it would heat rapidly. Then he looked up at Jack with, 'Thought you aimed to search the spread. Go ahead.'

Jack was silent.

'Go ahead.'

Jack caught the hidden anger in Ross Bassett's words. Bassett was his mortal enemy. Probably only the veiled threat of hidden riflemen on the hill kept Bassett from turning his own gun—and the guns of Triangle S riders—against him. He had ridden in here on a hunch. That hunch, he realized, was worthless.

Jack turned his bronc.

'So long, *tinhorn*.' Cynicism edged Bassett's harsh voice.

Jack let the cynicism ride. *Tinhorn* was a low word applied to a cheating gambler. This was no time to pick trouble. Nor any place, either. Of course, Bob Pasco was back in the brush, but Bob Pasco was only one man and one rifle. And here Bassett had many men . . . and many rifles.

There was no percentage in searching the Triangle S. He was sure Bassett was willing to let him search the spread. In fact, Bassett was too willing; his tone had been almost eager. Jack was sure a Triangle S man had been wounded. Sonny Doyle had shot a Bassett man.

A rider came out of the bunk-house. He saw Jack and started back, but it was too late. He stopped, looked at the merchant.

'We've met before, huh?' Jack tantalized him.

'Don't get rough.'

Jack said, 'Old Milo Dawson told me he had canned you, Rodtem. So you hit over here for a job, huh? Birds of a feather flock together.'

Rodtem's eyes were bloodshot. His lips and jaw showed the punishing effects of Jack's pounding fists. He moved over, steps short and stood beside Jack's horse, looking up with a controlled anger.

'Storekeeper, I oughta—'

A bullet smashed into the dust about fifteen feet to the right. It had been fired from one of the hills. Rodtem jumped, and Jack's horse moved quickly, also frightened. Ross Bassett had been hurrying toward them. Now Bassett stopped in his tracks, his mouth open slightly.

Jack's voice was cold. 'One of my farmers fired that rifle bullet. That was only a warning bullet. At that range they could kill every man-jack of you as you ran for cover.'

Ross Bassett swore. His voice was a monotone that spewed out curses. They were directed toward his guar. He blamed the man for letting five imaginary farmers get stationed on the hills. Of course, he figured the farmers were real, not figments of Jack's planning.

Bassett said angrily, 'Ride out of this outfit,

121

Farrell!'

'With pleasure.'

Jack rode past Rodtem. By this time the man's face had regained its ruddy color. Rodtem's eyes were still hot and angry. Jack raised the butt of his shot-leaded quirt, came down with it.

Rodtem tried to duck. The quirt smashed down, catching across the temple. Rodtem went back and landed in the dust. He didn't get up. Jack looked at Bassett.

'Tell him to keep a civil tongue after this.'

Again Bassett started forward, hand close to holstered .45. And again another rifle-ball smashed into the dust, lifting dirt about ten feet ahead of Ross Bassett. And again Bassett stopped, pulled his hand up.

'Get out,' he repeated.

Jack said, 'My men are covering me, so be careful.' He turned and rode away. Rodtem sat up, hands to his head.

'Be careful, Rodtem.' Bassett snapped the order.

It took all the nerve Jack had to make that ride. He put his bronc to a running-walk, back toward Bassett and his men. He had made a threat—an imagined threat—and only one rifle was there on the hill. And that rifle had spoken twice, and its threat was naked over the Triangle S owner and hands.

Jack Farrell had a cold spot up and down his spine. Any moment he expected a bullet to smash into his back. He knew that Bassett had hidden rifle-men. He knew that, if one of these men shot him, Bob Pasco—up there on that hill—would never be able to shoot the murderer, hidden as he was.

Pasco held only one good threat. And the threat was this: Ross Bassett stood in the open; if one of Bassett's riflemen shot, then Pasco would kill Bassett. And Bassett knew this, too.

'Nobody shoot,' Bassett roared. 'He rides out unharmed, men. Me, I'm in the open, and if one of you tag him—down I go. No shootin', savvy!'

Jack almost smiled. Ross Bassett's bellowing voice held fear, if he was any judge at recognizing fear in a voice. He reached the brush, made the turn in the trail; trees and brush hid him from the Triangle S. Only then did he feed his cayuse the spurs.

He roared down the trail, high in stirrups. Shale came down the slope, and behind it was Bob Pasco's mount. Pasco swung in, rowled his horse hard and caught up with Jack.

'Never seen nobody light out to follow you,' Pasco hollered. 'Still, we'd best put some miles between us an' them right fast.'

They loped hard, driving ponies, quirts working. Pasco reined close, yelled, 'Did I shoot at the right time?'

Jack said, 'You sure did, pard.' His hand grabbed the farmer's sleeve. 'You were five gunmen, savvy?'

'Five?' Pasco frowned.

They were on the basin bottom, and here it was level and they could have seen any pursuit behind them. So they pulled blowing mounts to a walk.

Jack told about the bluff he had pulled on the Triangle S men. And when Bob Pasco smiled, the smile held no mirth.

'Accomplish anythin', Jack?'

Jack leaned on one stirrup. 'The wounded man ain't on that ranch, Bob. Bassett told me I could search the place.'

'He mean that?'

Jack nodded.

Pasco said, 'If he wanted you to search, that was the same as tellin' you the wounded man wasn't there. Well, we know that, for certain; the ride did some good. 'Though it was danged risky . . . or so it turned out to be.'

Jack remembered the cold spot on his back when he had ridden away from the Bassett ranch. This farmer was right: the risk had been great. But it had, in its way, been worthwhile.

For one thing, he was sure that no wounded man was harbored at the Triangle S. Otherwise Bassett would not have been willing to let him search the buildings. That meant the wounded man had either died or ridden on. Either way, it made no difference.

Had the man been available, he'd have made him talk—and his evidence would have made the sheriff at Cody Point issue a warrant either for Dawson or Bassett. One of them had cut that fence.

Again, he eliminated old Milo Dawson. The old man had talked straight and square. All indications pointed to Bassett.

'If Dawson shows up at that farmer meetin',' Pasco cut in, 'us farmers'll know he's square t'ord us. It'll take guts for him to ride in there. Hope he comes alone. If he brings his riders, there might be trouble.'

'I was just thinking the same thing.'

Pasco fell back to nursing his thoughts. Jack also played with his thoughts. He had gained another point, too. Rodtem had been driven from the Rafter T; the cowhand had immediately ridden to the Triangle S.

That meant only one thing: Bassett had had Rodtem as a spy at the Milo Dawson spread. Jack smiled. When old Milo Dawson heard that news, he'd get hot under the collar for sure. Bassett had pulled a smart trick on the old cowman. Jack made sure he would get the news to Dawson, too.

This news—and the humiliation of harboring a Bassett spy—would drive old Milo even deeper in with the farmers, for it would directly increase his anger and antipathy towards Ross Bassett.

Jack was sure Rodtem had come out of that

125

bunkhouse by accident. Had Rodtem known he was on the premises he would never have blundered out where Jack could have seen him.

There was another element in his favor, also. He had called Ross Bassett—called Bassett on his own Triangle S ranch—and he had run a bluff on him. And what was more, the bluff had worked.

Word would get to the farmers about this bold ride right into Bassett's camp, how one man—a rifleman hidden on the hill—had tossed in two bullets to bluff Bassett and his hired gunhands. This story would brush aside most of the doubt the farmers had regarding his loyalty to them and their cause. Then, if Milo Dawson appeared at the farmers' meeting, and if Dawson made a convincing talk—his farmers would have to restore their faith in him. For Dawson would plainly show that he, Jack, did not favor the cowmen.

Dawson's appearance at the meeting would substantiate that point.

Jack sat sidewise in saddle, face grave. This day had seen a little progress made, but yet the problem had not found its only answer. Bassett would never give up, he knew.

'Where'll he hit next, Bob?'

Pasco looked at him. 'Who hit?'

'Bassett, of course.'

Pasco scowled, 'My dam, maybe?'

Jack rolled that thought. 'I believe that

126

would be the place.' He rubbed his jaw, slowly took his hand back. His jaw was sore. We'd best leave three guards, at least, there tomorrow night. Mayhenry, Sherman, Schell.'

'Why those three?'

Jack smiled, the smile thin. 'They trust me. I know that. The other farmers—them that don't trust me—had best be there. What about their cabins?'

'I've thought of that, too.'

Jack straightened, boots in stirrups. 'We'll get them to leave their big kids home to guard cabins and barns. Maybe we should hold the meeting in the afternoon? That would be daylight, and raiders might not be so apt to hit in the afternoon as at night. No night to cover them.'

'That'd be best.'

Jack said, 'I'll get word out to Milo Dawson.'

This settled, they put their ponies to a lope. They had covered many miles, weaving back and forth across Wild River Basin; their mounts were tired and needed oats and hay and the stable. Both of them were hungry. Pasco swung off at the fork with, 'Me for home, Jack.'

'Get word to the farmers about the meeting.'

Pasco nodded, very serious. 'Good luck, fella.'

Jack pushed on toward Wild City. Again, he checked the day and its events; he found nothing disturbing. Of course they had not found the wounded man; still, he'd set Billy Stebbins to watching the doctor's office and home. Mrs. Stebbins would help, too. And he could watch also. Or maybe Doc would work with them and report if a wounded man came in.

He'd ask him to do that.

The sun was at its hottest when he reached Wild City. His horse drank at the trough on the town's outskirts. A spring on the hill fed into a pipe and then carried water into the rock and concrete trough. His father had had that trough built to water horses of his customers.

Across the basin, devil-twists of dust played, sired by the drouth and heat. They played high into the sky, spiralling funnels of dust. Out of habit, Jack looked at the sky: it was brazen and hot and without clouds. The only coolness was the rim of snow on the western mountains.

He drew rein in front of the restaurant. He would eat, and Billy Stebbins would spot his horse, come after it and lead the critter to the barn. Mrs. Doyle sat on the shaded porch of the town hotel.

She looked at him, but did not speak. She was only about a hundred feet away, and he went toward the restaurant, the imprint of her gaze on him making him uncomfortable. She carried anger a long way, he realized.

Suddenly he stopped. Billy Stebbins had come out of the Mercantile. He came up to Jack's horse, then suddenly put his hand against the animal's sweaty shoulder. Jack heard his sobs.

Jack turned, walked to the sidewalk's rim, ever mindful of Mrs. Doyle's silent and watchful poise.

'What's the matter, Billy?'

'Sonny Doyle—he died!'

## CHAPTER ELEVEN

Grizzled old Milo Dawson walked the floor of his office, hands locked behind his back. A weight had left him, but still he was not happy. At heart, he was a sympathetic man: now he remembered Sonny Doyle down there in Wild City. Somebody had shot an innocent youth.

And that wasn't right. Men could fight over land and ideals, but there was no use in dragging the kids into it. The weight, therefore, was still there. And it hung there, despite the fact his two women-folk were at peace with him.

For he had told them more about his talk with Jack Farrell and Bob Pasco. Martha had, of course, listened in to the conversation; Mrs. Dawson had not, though. And old Milo found satisfaction in telling his wife what had happened.

'Thank the good Lord,' Ada Dawson had said.

She had sat there, an old woman broken by arthritis and rheumatism, but her face had been suddenly lighted, glowing with a mystic peace. And again old Milo felt the full impact of his wife's deep love for him.

'Are you happy now, Ada?' He'd made his voice gruff.

'Heavenly happy.' Ada had looked at Martha. 'I only have two fears now: one for Martha's Jack, and the other for this Doyle boy.'

Martha said, 'The Doyle boy isn't wounded badly, so Jack said. He's young and like rawhide, and Jack says Doc said he'd be well soon.'

'I wonder who shot him?' Ada Dawson drummed bent fingers on the wheels of her wheelchair.

'I don't know who shot him,' Milo Dawson said. 'But I know who ordered it, and that man was Ross Bassett.'

'He's a gunman,' Mrs. Dawson said slowly.

Martha's lovely face lost a little color. She had caught the full implication of her mother's slow words. Bassett was pitched against Jack Farrell, and Bassett was a deadly gunman.

'Jack can handle a gun,' she maintained.

Her father said, 'Not like—' and then Milo Dawson said no more. He kissed his wife on the cheek and went to his office, leaving his two women in the house. On the way he met a Rafter T cowpuncher.

'Phil, saddle a cayuse an' head into town. Stick around close, and if anythin' of importance happens, ride hell-fer-leather out to tell me.'

'Okay, Milo.'

The old cowman saddled his blue roan with a blazed face. He went into the barn and said to the hostler, 'Wanta take a ride with me, huh?'

'Where to, Milo?'

'Across the river. Over to the Bassett outfit.'

Old Tim peered up at him, leaning against his fork. 'Didn't figger you an' Ross Bassett was such lovin' friends, Milo, that you'd make that ride plumb acrost the Basin to blah with him?'

'I'm pullin' outa this trouble, Tim.'

A smile creased the wrinkled, wizened face. 'And am I danged happy to hear you got some sense at last, Milo! Bet your woman an' girl is happy. Now what for do you aim to talk about with Ross Bassett?'

'You're worse than an ol' woman. Get your mule an' saddle him or stay home. Take your pick. I give you ten minutes.'

Milo Dawson pulled out his big watch and timed his hired hand. It was all a joke, and both knew it. As it was, it took old Tim only seven minutes, and Milo Dawson pushed his watch into his pocket with, 'You're gettin' faster, young man. Come next stampede I'll enter you in the relay race down in Wild City. You're gettin' so you can saddle up right fast.'

'You ain't got no gun on you, nor no rifle in your saddle-holster.'

'Don't need none. You don't pack none either.'

Tim said, 'We might need irons.'

'Too danged many irons on this graze.' Dawson turned his horse and Tim gigged his mule close. They loped out of the ranch-yard, chickens running ahead of their mounts, the mule taking three jumps to two of Dawson's cayuse.

The scowl of puzzlement was plain on old Tim's face, and its confusion brought a hidden smile to Milo Dawson. Old Tim was wondering just what the boss of the Rafter T aimed to do over at the Bassett Triangle S. And Dawson let him keep on worrying.

They forded Wild River, came out onto grass claimed by Ross Bassett. A farmer came out of the buckbrush, riding a hop-shot old bay work-horse. The two Rafter T men pulled in.

'Done lost my milk cow this mornin',' the farmer said. 'See anythin' of a brockle-faced old cow acrost the river?'

'What brand?' Dawson asked.

'Out of state brand. Dakoty brand. Heart Slash Nine, big on the right ribs. Bought her at the Miles City auction.'

'She was about a mile south of the river,' Dawson said. 'Wanderin' south, too.'

'She's never crost that river before,' the farmer said. He looked at Milo Dawson. 'I was talkin' with Bob Pasco back yonder. He tol' me the meetin' has been set for tomorrow afternoon, 'stead of tomorrow night.'

'Good idea,' Dawson affirmed. 'I'll be there.'

'Dang glad to hear that. Now all we gotta fight is Bassett.'

'Yeah.' Tim unloaded a mouthful of tobacco juice. 'That's *all* you got to fight. Any more news?'

'Not that I know of.'

The two Rafter T men rode on, and behind them the farmer forded Wild River, muttering curses at a way-ward milk-cow who, had she heard them, would not have been in the least disturbed.

Finally Tim asked, 'What're we ridin' over to see Bassett about, boss?'

'I'm tellin' him I'm working with the farmers from here out,' Milo Dawson said. 'I'm warnin' him that if any other deviltry goes on his outfit will get full blame. I'm beginnin' to believe with my ol' lady: us cowmen can't whip these hoemen. We gotta work with them.'

'I knew you had the brains, but I never figured you'd get over your pride.'

Dawson sent a sharp glance towards his old hand. Tim had worked with him so many years neither could remember how long. But Old Tim, if he noticed the sharp glance, paid it no nevermind. He looked ahead, jaw pushed out with fine-cut teeth working like a beaver cutting off a log.

Ross Bassett and his men were just finishing putting the brand on the last colt. He looked up from his fire, recognized them, nodded. Then he carried his iron across the corral. The colt whinnied, the iron cut him; smoke trickled upward with its tell-tale odor of burned hair and hide.

'Turn him loose,' Bassett ordered his men.

The Triangle S boss came back to where Dawson and Tim sat their broncs outside the corral. He climbed over the corral with, 'Howdy, men. Strayed off'n your home-grass a little, huh?'

'We ain't got no home-grass,' Dawson said.

Bassett put his thick legs wide and studied the old man. Bassett's coarse face still showed the effects of the hammering fists of Jack Farrell. 'That's your opinion, Dawson. You kowtowin' down in front of these hoemen?'

134

Dawson said stiffly, 'I don't bow before nobody, an' you know it, Bassett. But I've seen the light. Nobody can have grounds to accuse me of shootin' a boy in the night while I cut his fence. Them farmers are meetin' tomorrow afternoon at their church.'

'Where do I fit in?'

Dawson spoke quietly, persuasively. 'Ross, me an' you have never been what a man would call good neighbors. We've had our differences. But all cowmen have them. Now I'm appealin' to your better judgment, Ross. Why don't you take in that meetin' tomorrow an' bury the hatchet with these sodmen?'

Bassett's hands were listening. Bassett looked at them and said in surprise, 'My Lord, who'd ever figure to hear them words from Cowman Milo Dawson?' He looked back to Dawson. 'They'll take your range if you don't fight.'

Dawson chewed, and a smile touched him. 'Come to think of it, Ross, I never did have no range.'

'What'd you mean? You ran cattle on grass, didn't you? You were the first man to run cattle on that land.'

'I know that. But I don't own that land. An' ol' man down in Washington owns it; he's owned it all this time. Now he wants to give it away, an' Uncle Sam don't want to give it to me; he wants farmers on it. I finally got wise. I'm stakin' my punchers out on

135

homesteads around what choice spots are left.'

'I've got men picking homesteads, too.'

Dawson chewed and Old Tim chewed and Ross Bassett watched them. Finally Dawson said, 'Good work, Ross. I come over here to tell you I'm pullin' outa this trouble. I'm tellin' the farmers that in the mornin' an' at that meetin' tomorrow.'

The implication was clear. From now on, if any trouble occurred, it would naturally be blamed on Bassett and his Triangle S riders.

'Thanks.' Bassett was very cynical.

'Well, we see eye to eye . . . on some matters.' Dawson turned his bronc and then, as an afterthought, added, 'That Doyle kid stopped a bullet, I understand.'

Bassett was rock-hard. Dawson knew either Bassett, or a Triangle S gunman, had cut that fence, shot the boy. But Bassett did not show it.

'Too bad, Milo.'

Old Tim waited, chewing quietly, sitting his mule. Dawson said, 'A farmer back yonder said my old hand, Rodtem, is workin' for you now. I canned him, and he came right over here and went to work, the farmer said.'

More implication. Actually Milo Dawson was saying, 'You had a spy in my camp. I fired him and he came home.'

Bassett was still stone-hard. 'Never knew that when I hired him,' he murmured. 'Well,
136

ride a tight saddle, Dawson.'

'Same to you.'

They rode for a mile in silence, and then old Tim said, 'You ran the he-coon up a cottonwood, Milo. You pushed the hand over to him, but he wouldn't pick up the cards.'

'He's dangerous and smart.'

'Not as smart as he is dangerous,' the hostler corrected.

Dawson had no reply to that. For some reason, he felt lighter and in better health than he'd felt for days. He ran back along the string of events, seeking for his lightness; he found it. He had pulled out of what was a dangerous fight. His withdrawal, due to his wife, daughter, and Jack Farrell, had been not too embarrassing. He was sitting on the outside now, watching—he wasn't fighting now.

'A man is a greedy fool, Tim.'

'You jus' findin' that out?'

Dawson spat out his chew. 'Like I told Bassett, we'll stake men on claims. They can file, prove up, get their deeds, then bind them over to me for payin' them wages while they homesteaded for me. That way I can take control of choice grass an' water an' I'll own it legally, not by squatter's rights.'

'I don't like the idea.'

'Why?'

'I might get stuck on a homestead.'

Dawson said, 'You will, don't worry. But

137

shucks, man, you only have to live on it six months of the year. That's all the law requires.'

'Six months is a long time. Mind one time I was in the calaboose up in Butte. Nine months, I got; it weren't my fault, either. I was standin' in the Silver Dollar, jus' a innercent bystander, when a struggle started—'

Milo Dawson did not listen. Only too often did old Tim go off on a wild bronc. Nobody paid any attention to him any longer. One time a cowboy had done some arithmetic and found out that old Tim was one hundred and forty-eight years old. Old Tim had bridled, instantly on guard.

'I don't tell nobody my age,' the hostler had said. 'You ain't even close, cowboy. No man lives to be as ol' as you claim I am. How come you arrive at such a conclusion?'

The cowboy had explained. According to Tim, he had worked sixteen years in the Butte coppermines; he'd driven Wells-Fargo stage for twenty-three years; he left Pennsylvania when he was sixteen; he'd punched cows in Arizona Territory for eighteen years.

'I added them all up,' the cowboy said. 'I sat and listened to your windies, and I took note of each job: you're one hundred and forty-eight years old.'

'Humph . . .'

Now, with old Tim starting out on another windy, Milo Dawson paid him no heed. The cowman found himself wondering just what Ross Bassett would do. He put himself in Bassett's boots and tried to figure from the viewpoint of the Triangle S owner. And that wasn't hard.

Bassett had not shown his true feelings when he and Tim had talked to the cowman. Dawson knew Bassett had been seething inside. He had ridden to the Triangle S to put his cards on the table, to show Bassett he could expect no co-operation against the nesters from the Rafter T. This he had done, and Bassett had taken it with a stoic cynicism.

Maybe Bassett would fight two combines now: the farmers and the Rafter T. But Dawson found himself doubting the possibility that Bassett might work against the Rafter T. For one thing, Bassett had his hands full, just fighting the farmers. So Milo Dawson discredited the theory that Bassett might do dirty work against his outfit.

For years he had watched Ross Bassett closely. At one time, about a decade ago, he had figured he had been losing cattle; he'd put a close eye on Bassett's outfit. But evidently his tally count had been short. For he could get no proof of Bassett rustling Rafter T beef.

Would Bassett hit at the big dam being built by Bob Pasco? Dawson thought, That'd

139

be the right place to hit; the logical place. He played with this, and then Tim said, 'What would you have done, Milo?'

'I'd've killed him,' Dawson said emphatically.

Tim eyed him belligerently, his jaw working. 'Why, you weren't even listenin' to a man! This ain't a matter of killin' nobody! I put the question up about the time that hoss stampeded with me down in New Mexico Territory—done took the bit in his jaws an' froze it—Ah, no use talkin' to you; you're too ol' to think or hear!'

'I agree with you.'

Tim fell to nursing his thoughts in silence. One way to get the garrulous oldster to quit talking was to agree with him. If a man got into an argument with him he played into Tim's hands. Tim could and would argue about anything at any place and at any time of the day or night.

They put their mounts to a lope, the mule a pace behind. The afternoon was almost gone when they reached the ford in Wild River. Phil, the cowpuncher Dawson had dispatched into Wild City, was watering his bronc there.

'What's news?' Dawson asked.

Phil said, 'Pasco and Jack Farrell are lookin' for the man who killed Sonny Doyle. The town is hot, some for the farmers, some—'

'The man who what?'

'The kid, Dawson. He died.'

'Died?'

Tim asked, 'That bullet—it was in his shoulder, weren't it? How could he die from that?'

'I'm no doc.' Phil spread his hands. 'Doc says that a piece of the lead got into his veins. A sharp piece, he claims; it hit the kid's heart—went through his blood stream.'

Milo Dawson said, 'Well, I'll be—' He looked at his two men solemnly. 'Lord, that'll rip the lid off hell, men!'

'Trouble to pay,' Phil said.

## CHAPTER TWELVE

Doc said, 'I thought he was all right, Jack. His pulse was good, and his temperature was all right—then he just died. I made an autopsy.'

The medico's blunt, short fingers handed Jack a small, sharp piece of lead. Jack looked at it, feeling its keenness.

'That must've broken off the shell,' Doc said. 'I found it in his heart.' The doctor looked at his hands. 'Life isn't worth much, is it?' He answered his own question. 'One little bit of sharp lead, just under the aorta, and the boy was gone.' He shook his head slowly.

Jack stood there, turning the sharp piece between thumb and forefinger. He remembered Mrs. Doyle sitting there on the hotel porch as he had ridden into town. Now he knew why her eyes had been so dull, so heavy, as they had settled on him. Now he knew why her slow gaze had followed him as he had dismounted in front of the restaurant.

Grief had bent her, and, in the bending, grief had warped her perspective. The woman needed some person or thing upon which to blame her grief, and she had selected Jack because he had moved her family and husband into Wild River Basin. And that, Jack thought, was not just.

Doc said, 'She blames you, Jack.'

Jack said, 'What can I do?' How can a man tell another he is deadly sick inside, and that the sickness cannot be cured by medicine? Something in his words, in his eyes, told the medico his trouble.

'Nothing, I guess. I talked with her. She blames you. I told her to curse the man who had placed the bullet against the boy. She looked at me with dull, stupid eyes. She hasn't too much mentality, Jack. What little she has she refuses to use.'

'How about Mike Doyle?'

'Angry and hurt.'

Jack felt his own anger flare. 'Why do they blame me, the fools? I never shot their kid! Mike Doyle should have known better than to

142

let a hot-tempered kid run a night-guard!' He caught himself. He walked to the window and looked out on Wild City's main street.

Just a dusty, dirty stretch of dust. No ruts, for rain had been months—or was it years?—ago; ruts had worn down under rims of wagons and the hoofs of horses. Only a common street.

But what about the men and women and children who crossed it, who traveled along it with rigs? Or the countless generations to come—people who would never know the names of the men who fought here for freedom? Was it something handed down, this heritage of land?

Jack said, 'Sorry, Doc.'

'The blow-off did you good.' The medico cleaned an instrument. 'Now what, if anything, did you find at the Rafter T or the Triangle S?'

'Bassett stands tough and hard. He won't change. It's between him and me now. The next time we meet there'll be a showdown, and if the odds favor Bassett, there'll be the finish. I'm sure of that.'

'And Milo Dawson?'

Jack said, 'Dawson's breaking in two. In fact, he has broken. We can lay most of that to Martha and Ada Dawson. He's coming to the meeting tomorrow afternoon. Dawson is neutral now.'

'I thought he could read the writing.'

Jack told about how he and Bob Pasco had trailed the wounded man to the Post Hole Creek line-camp. He told about his run-in with Rodtem, and how Rodtem had gone over to the Triangle S.

'He's shifty.'

Jack said suddenly, 'Have you treated a wounded man in the last few hours, Doc?'

The medico studied him. 'Only Sonny Doyle.'

'I said a *man*,' Jack pointed out. 'Not a boy.'

The doctor had evaded his question; both knew this. That was the reason Jack Farrell was so specific.

'I can't tell you that, Jack.' The medico pointed to his framed oath on the wall. 'I have to be true to that.'

'Hogwash!' Jack snorted the words. 'It's your own stubborn pride. You medicos break that cheap oath a dozen times a day!'

'I can't tell you.'

Jack said, 'All right. But from now on your office is going to be watched, both front and back doors. When and if you leave town, a man will be trailing you, and you can be danged sure of that, Doc.'

'I thought you had enough trouble?'

'I can handle more,' Jack said.

He went outside, a dozen emotions mingling in him. He had tipped his hand, but what other recourse had he had? None! From now it was dog snap at dog, dog chew dog. His ride into the Triangle S had driven Ross Bassett flatly against him. And coupled with the effrontery of his ride into Bassett's lair was the added stigma of Bob Pasco's bullets whamming into the ground in front of Bassett. Bassett had lost face there, and his face had shown it by its dark anger.

Dusk was here, and Jack did not feel its coolness. He was hot inside, and this heat flushed his face. Mrs. Doyle had left the porch of the hotel, evidently because of the encroaching coolness of night, and he was glad for that. In his present mood a word from the woman would have driven him to say something perhaps he would later have regretted.

He was standing there, gathering his temper, when Mike Doyle came up, coming out of the Mercantile.

Mike Doyle said hoarsely, 'Damn you, Farrell!' He was wild and he hit, but Jack moved back. The man's knuckles nicked Jack's jaw. Doyle swore and came in, and Jack knocked him back against the store.

Doyle remained against the wall, dark and short and stocky. Blood came from the corner of his mouth; he worked his teeth.

Jack said, 'You've drunk too much.'

The blow seemed to have sobered the farmer. His hand came up, the back of it wiping his mouth. He looked at Jack again.

145

This time the fury had left and his eyes were a little stunned.

'Jack, I'm sorry.'

Jack said, 'Forget it,' and walked into his store. Down the street two farmers stood and watched, and Jack caught the cynical edges of their scrutiny. He locked the door behind him and went through the gathering darkness to his office. There he lighted the lamp and found his chair.

He glanced through his mail. He didn't open a letter; he just looked at the return addresses. Another letter from another wholesale house. One held the railroad's address. He opened it, read it, tossed it aside.

A key turned in the front. Mrs. Stebbins came in, Billy with her. Jack told them about his talk with Doc. Mrs. Stebbins said, 'From my back window. I can watch tonight. But I won't be much 'count tomorrow in the store.'

'I'll get Mrs. Jones to help,' Jack said. He looked at Billy. 'But there's no use watching the front of the office, is there? Doc lives in the back. If somebody came at night, they'd come to the back and you could see the light go on in Doc's quarters where he sleeps.'

Billy said, 'I'll watch the office good tomorrow.'

Jack ran over this plan and found it good. Mrs. Stebbins kept glancing at the letter from the railroad.

'The railroad has shut down grade work for

the rest of this year,' Jack explained. 'The money panic has broken a little, but it's too late in the summer to start a crew working again.'

'Oh.'

'The letter indicates they might go across Wild River Basin, too. Surveys have been made of the Missouri River route, and the grade will be easier to build through Wild River.'

'That's good.'

Jack said, 'It doesn't mean much. One of those big supers can change it in the flash of what he'd call an idea. But we have to work and hope. If these farmers'll stay, I think we'll have rails through here by a year from this fall.'

'I sure hope so. Have you eaten, Jack?'

Jack shook his head.

She started a fire in the stove, fried eggs, made coffee. Billy sat down gladly for his second supper. When they were in the middle of the meal somebody knocked at the front door. Billy answered and came back with Martha Dawson behind him. Martha said, 'Too late for chuck?'

'Gag Billy,' Jack said, 'and there might be a little left for you.'

Billy said, 'Thanks, *friend*.'

Martha sat down, smoothing her buckskin riding-skirt. Jack thought, She makes a picture . . . and a danged lovely one, too.

Martha said, 'I was talking with Mrs. Pasco, Jack. Every farmer seems happy to think Dad won't buck them any longer.'

'Not as happy as I am.'

Martha had visited with other farmers, too. Warmness filled Jack, flowing into the old cavity left by Sonny Doyle's death. Martha had been out working for him among the wives of the farmers. She had done everything she could to lighten his load.

'You're swell, Martha,' Billy Stebbins said.

'More than swell,' Jack corrected him. 'Wonderful.'

Martha said, 'Don't talk that way.'

Mrs. Stebbins poured her a cup of coffee. Jack ate, liking his food. Billy said, 'I wish Ross Bassett would get some sense, and would get out while the gettin' was good.'

Jack said, 'Too late for that.'

Martha and Mrs. Stebbins exchanged glances. Somebody had wounded Sonny Doyle, and Sonny had died, and Sonny would have had many, many days ahead of him. Sonny should have had the God-given right of growing up to be a man.

Jack knew that Mrs. Stebbins and Martha were worried about him. One with a maternal, mother-hen worry for a man who was her son in everything but blood; the other for the man who would marry her and who would become the father of her children. But he had fought this problem out of his own mind. He had made his compromise and this compromise demanded that he did not bow before Ross Bassett.

Once this argument had been concerned only over the right to graze cattle on Wild River Basin. At that time it had been an impersonal battle concerned with inanimate objects. Then Bassett had broken that barrier and brought a personal touch into it. He had fought with Jack and somebody—either Bassett or one of his men—had shot and killed Sonny Doyle.

Jack compared it to a giant spotlight. The carbide-light had first shone all over the Basin, flooding it with a dull light. Then with the passage of days it had narrowed and pulled down into a spotlight that shone on two men only: Jack and Ross Bassett.

Once there had been three men, and at that time old Milo Dawson had been within the confining cone of light. But Dawson, by his own admission, had pulled back into the dark; now only Bassett and Jack occupied that dangerous circle.

'We'll meet it when and if it comes,' Jack philosophized.

The women exchanged glances. 'That's all we can do,' Martha said. She got to her feet. 'Well, I'm tired, Jack. No, I'm not riding to the ranch tonight. I'm staying with Millie Stevens tonight.'

Jack followed her to the front door. He

kissed her and held her, her body warm against him, her lips moist. He whispered, 'Good gosh, what would I do without you?' and his voice was boyish.

'Jack, please be careful.'

'I sure will, Martha.'

Then she was gone and he clicked shut the night latch and went back to his office. Mrs. Stebbins was gathering the dirty plates. 'I'll take these home and wash them. Jack, what do you think?'

Jack bluffed. 'Think about what?'

The woman looked over the dirty dishes at him. 'You know what I'm talking about! Poor Martha, she's scared to death. Word has gone around that Bassett claims that the next time you and he meet it'll be a gunfight. You know that, Jack.'

Jack was very sober. 'I sure do, Nellie.' Then he spread his fingers suggestively and smiled. 'But I won't run, you can bet on that.'

'I'm afraid, Jack.'

'Don't be, please.'

'Jack can take care of himself,' Billy said in a worldly manner. 'And besides, I'll side him with my .22 rifle!'

'Billy, hush!'

'These women, Jack! All the same, no matter how old they are!'

'That's right,' Jack said.

He was letting Mrs. Stebbins and her son

out the front door when Doc came out of the darkness. Doc said, 'If anybody shows up wounded, I'll let you know. I got to thinking of young Sonny.'

Jack murmured, 'Thanks.' Then to Mrs. Stebbins, 'That means a night of sleep for you, Nellie.'

'I won't be able to sleep.'

The woman and son moved into the night. Doc stood sucking his cigar, his breath heavy.

Wild City was slow and sluggish, warm in the night. Lights were out in business establishments, but the smithy was shoeing a horse, the scene lighted by the lantern hanging from the nail in the post.

Doc said, 'If that danged idiot pounds nails all night like he did last night, I'll climb out of bed and beat him to death with his own hammer. He's so busy shoeing work-horses for the farmers, and he's so greedy for a dollar, that he works all night, keeping all peaceful citizens awake.'

Jack said, 'My gosh, you're touchy.'

Doc said gruffly, 'We're all touchy. The whole danged passel of us idiots are on edge.' He walked off, the tip of his cigar glowing.

'You're right,' Jack silently agreed.

# CHAPTER THIRTEEN

Jack called, 'Hello, the house.' The Doyle
dog barked, jumping up on Jack's horse's
shoulder, and the horse squared around,
aiming to kick the cur. Mike Doyle came out
of the barn.

'Get down, Mutt!'

The dog kept on jumping. Doyle took a
kick at the canine, caught the dog in the
rump. The dog ran off and crawled under the
porch. Doyle looked up at Jack Farrell, and
the farmer wore a scowl.

'What'd you want, Jack?'

Jack said, 'I thought maybe you'd ride to
the meeting with me, Mike. I want you to
take my hand, friend. I'm terribly sorry about
last night.'

Mike Doyle's bottom lip twitched. He
looked at the house, then back at Jack. His
voice trembled. 'Jack, you shouldn't've been
the one to apologize. Good Lord, man, I
never got to sleep last night. Forgive an old
fool, Jack? With all my heart, I ask that.'

Jack dismounted and put his arm around
the Irishman's blocky shoulders. 'My fault,
Mike. Now let's go into the house and see
your missus.'

'She feels better this morning.'

Mrs. Doyle and her daughter were doing

the dishes. The little girl's eyes were red, Jack noticed. The woman regarded him in stony silence. Mike Doyle wiped a tear from his eye.

Jack said, 'Mrs. Doyle, I came to take Mike to the meeting.'

'That is good,' she said. 'I didn't want him to go alone.'

'I was just harnessin' my team,' Doyle cut in. 'We'll go over on horseback, huh, instead of the buckboard?'

'Whichever way you want,' Jack said.

'A cup of coffee, Mr. Farrell.' Mrs. Doyle poured three cups. Doyle went to the cupboard and came back with a quart of Old Folsom. He spiked each drink, and Mrs. Doyle sat beside Jack.

'It is sorry, sir, that I am.'

Jack said, 'I know how you felt. I think we each misjudged the other, Mrs. Doyle. I'm only doing what little God will let me do. It isn't much. I wish it were more.'

'I'm sorry I doubted you, Mr. Farrell.'

Jack felt much better. He didn't mention Sonny or the fact that Sonny would be buried in the morning. They finished their coffee and Jack felt the bite of the whiskey. Before they left, Doyle took another long drink from the bottle. Then he and Jack unharnessed the team, saddled one of the horses, and the two of them rode toward the church.

Doyle said, 'The missus has a good heart,

153

Jack. But it hit her hard; her oldest child.'

Jack nodded. There was nothing he could say. By this time word would have passed around through the farmers telling about how he and Bob Pasco had braced the Triangle S men. Pasco would see it got around.

His sagging stock had evidently picked up strength during the night. By bracing Ross Bassett in his lair he had shown the farmers he meant business. But he had also made a greater enemy out of Bassett.

He dallied with the latter thought. Maybe he had done wrong, at that? Maybe Ross Bassett would have seen the light—as old Milo Dawson had seen the light—and maybe Bassett would have joined the farmers. But since he had been challenged, right in his home ranch—?

Jack knew this was only wishful thinking. Even if he had not challenged Bassett, the Triangle S man would have still bucked the farmers. He had done one definite thing, though: he had eased the pressure on his farmers. For by jumping on Bassett, he had turned Bassett's entire antipathy toward himself, thereby taking the pressure off his hoemen.

'Sure glad Milo Dawson's joined us,' Doyle said.

'He ain't joined us,' Jack corrected. 'He's just sitting on one side and being neutral, that's all.'

'That's about as good,' Mike Doyle conceded.

The wind murmured through sagebrush and grease-wood, singing a song that would still be sung when the last man had been and gone. They were along the rim of the foothills, and a cottontail rabbit darted up into the rocks toward his den, his white tail bobbing in his hurry. He had been feeding around a spring where there was a little green grass.

'We get plenty of dams built, Jack, and this basin'll be a garden, I tell you. This soil will raise anything if it has the water.'

'We'll get water to it.'

They met a rider on Swan Creek. Jack knew him as Milt Stuart, a Bassett Triangle S hand. Stuart said, 'Howdy, men,' and added: 'You ridin' my way?'

Jack said, 'We're heading for the meeting at the church.'

'That's my destination, too.'

Jack looked questioningly at Mike Doyle. Doyle did not hide his surprise that a Bassett rider should attend a farmers' meeting.

'I don't foller you, Stuart.' Doyle spoke slowly. 'You're on Ross Bassett's payroll. If'n he wanted to know what was goin' on at the meetin', why didn't he come hisself? Jack done invited him.'

Stuart smiled. He was a bony man who smiled easily. He made no enemies, wanted no enemies, and wanted no trouble. He shrugged. 'I don't know a danged thing about it, Doyle. All I know is that Bassett ordered me to attend this meetin', if you farmers'll let me in. I'm not fightin' or gettin' into a mess just to carry out the boss's orders. But Bassett wants me to report back to him . . . if'n you gents'll let me attend.'

'You'll attend,' Jack said. 'I'd rather Bassett get a clear report of the meeting from one of his own men than to have him get a distorted, third hand version. You figure Bassett aims to give in?'

Again Milt Stuart shrugged. 'I don't know, Jack. I just work for the Triangle S. Each month Bassett pays my wages. He gives me top wages for my job. I've worked there ten years or more. I never ask no questions, but take my orders and do my job if possible.'

Mike Doyle growled, 'That scissorbill just wants information, Jack! He's afraid to come hisself, so he sends a hand of his!'

Stuart smiled, shrugged, was silent.

Jack said, 'Milt'll have plenty to tell him, once the meeting is over. Yonder comes two horsemen.'

'Old Milo and his daughter,' Milt Stuart said.

Dawson looked at Stuart and said, 'Reppin' for Bassett, huh?' and Stuart nodded. Jack and Martha rode stirrup to stirrup, well behind the three men. Jack put his hand over

156

Martha's and kissed her quickly, leaning from the saddle.

'Jack, they might look around. I'd be so embarrassed.'

Jack said, 'Ah, pshaw,' and kissed her again, only not so quickly this time. Then he sat straight in the saddle. He was scowling again, and Martha asked, 'What are you thinking about?'

'Nothing.'

'You're fibbing, Jack.'

Jack spread his hands in mock disgust. 'Lord, what a hen-pecked married life I'll lead,' he told the wind. 'Yes, I'm thinking of something, but I'm going to spring it at the meeting, not now.'

'Hope it's a good idea.'

'All my ideas are good, chicken.'

'Humph!'

They rode in silence, their horses at a quick walk. Jack realized he was glad Ross Bassett had sent Stuart to the meeting. He only hoped the farmers would let Stuart attend. Some of them would undoubtedly claim Stuart was only a spy for Bassett. Which, in reality, he was.

But still, Jack had invited Bassett to the meeting. Old Milo Dawson had also asked Bassett to make his appearance. But Jack hardly blamed Ross Bassett for not attending himself.

For one thing, personal feeling ran high

against Bassett, and if the cowman had attended in person, there might have been trouble. Jack knew also that Bassett would not bend. The presence of Milt Stuart was not a concession on Bassett's part. Milt Stuart was here as a reporter. He'd listen, then report back to his boss. Which was all right, Jack figured.

'What if you want a closed session with the farmers?' Martha asked. 'What about Milt Stuart then?'

'He'll leave when he's asked to.'

'Bassett sent the right man. Stuart's level-headed and will sidestep trouble. For once Bassett used his brains.'

'He's smart enough,' Jack assured her.

The church also served as a school house. It was set on the flat above Trout Creek, now a dry stream because of the drouth. Quite a number of rigs and saddle-horses were tied to the hitchrack. Jack took a mental count and said, 'A few more left to trek in. Some are always late.'

Milo Dawson and Mike Doyle and Milt Stuart had already tied up their broncs. They were standing with a group and a farmer was talking, using his hands a lot. One farmer came up to Jack, lifting his hat to Martha.

'What's that Bassett hand doin' at our meetin'?'

Jack said, 'Don't worry, fellow.'

'He come to start trouble?'

Jack shook his head. 'And don't any of you farmers start any trouble, either. Mind that, now?'

The man grunted something and walked away. Jack noticed all the farmers wore guns. On some the weapons looked decidedly out of place. He grinned as he thought, Bet some could stand inside a chicken-coop without windows and with the doors closed, and they couldn't hit a wall. But that thought was far from pleasant. When it came to a showdown, his men wouldn't be of much account.

But the merchant had taken this into account months before, so the thought was not too disturbing now. He noticed that Milo Dawson took out his watch, studied it, then glanced inquiringly at him.

'It's time, Jack.'

Jack hollered, 'Everybody inside.'

They trooped in with very little horseplay. Jack counted them as they entered, and found one missing. 'Where's Mayhenry?'

'On guard. Up on the hill.'

Jack nodded. 'Good idea. You report back to him, Jones, and tell him what happened at this meeting?'

'That I will, Jack.'

Reverend Mitchell opened the meeting with a short prayer. Martha played the organ and sang a hymn. Old Milo Dawson's voice, clear and strong, hovered over the voices of the farmers. Martha's voice was clear and calm. Even Milt Stuart sang.

Jack called the meeting to order, walked to the window and looked out, deliberately letting silence grow. Then he introduced Milt Stuart who stood up in acknowledgement.

'You spyin' for Bassett, fella?'

The farmer's voice was hot. Jack pounded on his desk and said, 'Who said that?' Mack Schell stood up. Jack said, 'This is an organized meeting, Mr. Schell. Abide by the rules. If you or anybody wants to speak, I'll recognize you and then you can have the floor. What's your question?'

'What's Stuart doing here?'

Stuart said, 'Mr. Farrell, let me explain my stand.'

Milt Stuart repeated the same thing he had told Jack. He had come merely to attend and report back the happenings to Ross Bassett. He knew nothing beyond his orders, and if further questions were to be asked, they should be asked of his boss, Ross Bassett.

'I apologize,' Mack Schell said.

'And I accept, Mr. Schell.'

Schell and Stuart sat down. Jack summed up the situation: he told about the railroad's plans, the Eastern money panic's effect on them, how the wholesalers were pushing him, and finally he got down to the fact that, to defend themselves, they could not look to the sheriff's office in Cody Point, or to the Territorial Governor for the militia.

'Any suggestions, men?'

Eli Sherman got to the floor. 'We organize our own militia, Jack. They did it during the War for Freedom and we can do it here. I move we band, arm, and become known as a peaceful body, going under the name our forefathers went under: the Minute Men.'

Jack had had that idea in mind. Now he acted as if he had not thought of it. 'Anybody second it?'

'I second it,' Milo Dawson said. He looked around from his shaggy height. 'That is, if you men'll accept my second.'

'We sure will, Milo.'

The meeting had suddenly turned into a grim and deadly council of war. Jack glanced at Martha, sitting in the front row by Mike Doyle, and he noticed the lack of color in her face. Her eyes met his. They were level eyes, and they gave him encouragement.

By unanimous vote the farmers organized into a militia. When the next farmer was molested, they would ride in a body for the Triangle S. One man—rawboned, stooped—asked for the floor.

'And Mr. Stuart—' A lean, gnarled finger pointed at the Triangle S man. '—I want you to so report to Mr. Bassett, your employer. I repeat again for your benefit and clearness: If a farmer gets shot, or a fence cut, we ride and raid the Triangle S. Your boss has men. But we outnumber them and we have the Law of

God with us, the Law of Righteousness.'

'Amen, Brother,' intoned Reverend Mitchell.

Stuart was impassive, his face without thoughts. The farmers had made a momentous decision—a decision that might leave some of their wives widows, their children fatherless. These thoughts were with Stuart when he looked at Jack Farrell's grim visage.

For once, all the hoemen were behind Jack. That thought was warm and yet, in its core, was iciness. Organization of the Minute Men as an open declaration of war against Bassett. These men had reached the end of their patience. They would sacrifice their families and homes—even their lives—to bring peace to Wild River Basin.

They decided on a meeting-place in case trouble broke out. They would ride from that point armed and ready. Stuart had gone outside by request, for Jack did not believe it right that the Bassett man should know the spot where they would meet. There was nothing else to discuss. Reverend Mitchell again prayed, his voice low and full. No more hymns were sung. The mood was hard, not one for music.

The farmers trooped out. Not much was said until the men were outside. Even then the conversation did not last long. They got into rigs, climbed on horses, and went toward their homes.

Mayhenry rode down the hill, coming out of the brush with his rifle over the saddle ahead of him. Jones met him and they rode away, with Jones explaining what had taken place at the meeting.

Bob Pasco said, 'Good job, Jack.'

'We'll stick together,' Jack assured him.

Pasco rubbed his hands together. 'I sure hope, though, it don't end in a pitched fight. You gettin' word to the governor we organized?'

'I'll send a man out of town for Cody Point. He'll send a wire to the governor and he'll give a written message to the sheriff. I kinda think this will drive both offices into some kind of action.'

'If it ain't too late by then.'

Jack said, 'Cheerful cuss, ain't you?'

Pasco mounted. 'Got to get back to my dam, Jack. The missus and my boy is guardin' it from the hill. I'd like to see anybody sneak past that woman. Cain't be done.'

Milo Dawson and Martha rode up. Dawson said, 'You had a good meetin', Jack. I think you jarred lots of us loose, fellow. One thing is, if word gets to the governor and sheriff that you farmers are making your own law because of lack of protection—well, somethin'll happen, I think.'

'I sure hope so,' Martha said.

Jack gave the girl a long look. 'Good for you, Martha. Yes, it might help us, at that.'

They rode away. A farmer cramped his rig short, the front wheel lifting the box, and another farmer said, with appropriate horseplay, 'You'll tip the whole thing over, Clem!'

'Go sell eggs, Joe.'

Jack waited until his farmers had all departed. Rigs were moving across the Basin, small against the sky and wide expanse. Milt Stuart came up leading his bronc. He and Jack were alone.

'Jack, I got something I want to say to you.'

'Go ahead, Milt.'

Stuart looked at his hands. 'I waited until they were all gone, especially Martha. I wouldn't want to hear. Of course, Ross Bassett sent me over here to attend the meeting, but he also had another reason for sending me.'

'Yes?'

Stuart lifted his eyes. His tongue wet his lips. 'Bassett'll never move against your Minute Men, Jack. Anyway, if he does, you won't be heading them, or so he will say when I tell him.'

Jack waited, cold inside.

Stuart wet his lips again. 'Bassett told me, above all other things, to get this word to you: the next time he meets you it'll be guns between you.'

'I'll be in town,' Jack said. 'Tell him that, Milt.'

'I'll tell him.'

Stuart found his stirrup, rode away. Jack watched him go but he did not see him. He was thinking of Wild City's dusty, narrow main street.

## CHAPTER FOURTEEN

Milt Stuart said, 'They organized what they call the Minute Men, Ross.'

'And then?'

'The minute you or your men move against one of them, the others are comin' to side him. They made themselves up a militia.'

Ross Bassett watched him with unblinking eyes. 'Go on, Stuart.'

'There ain't no more.' Stuart shrugged.

'You talk with Jack Farrell?'

Stuart reined his bronc toward the barn. 'Yeah, I talked to him. Told him what you told me: shootin' war from here out.' Ross Bassett followed his man into the barn where Milt Stuart dismounted. The man known as Rodtem had seen Stuart ride in, and he had left the bunkhouse and now he stood beside Bassett and listened. 'He said he'd be in town, Farrell did.'

Rodtem looked at Bassett. 'Things are shapin' up, huh?' he murmured. It was a question, but he did not expect an answer.

Stuart stripped gear from his bronc, hung up his saddle on the peg, kicked off his leather chaps and hung them over his saddle. He said, 'Me for some coffee,' and left.

Rodtem asked, 'What's in the wind, Ross?'

Bassett told him about the Minute Men. 'They're tied together now, Rodtem. We hit one and they'll tie in and raid us, so Stuart said.'

'What's wrong with that? It's about man to man, ain't it?'

Bassett said, 'Yeah, man to man. But how about old Milo Dawson and his hands? Martha's going to marry Farrell. Old Milo's signed up with the farmers, a man might say. He don't love me.'

Rodtem drew the toe of his right boot through the dust. A rooster crowed, standing up high. Rodtem said, 'A cock crowed at dawn,' and wondered where the phrase came from. He said, 'There must be a way, Ross.'

'There is.'

'And what is it?'

Bassett said one word, 'Farrell.'

Rodtem looked idly at the bunkhouse. 'He'll be in town without his farmers, too. They'll have gone to their farms. He's the head of the snake. Chop off that head, and the body might wiggle—but not for long.'

Bassett nodded. He was looking ahead, balancing these things; the scale tipped the wrong way. Rodtem was correct: Jack Farrell was the head. Bassett said, 'With Farrell gone—killed—the farmers'll be lost. Their women'll holler an' out they go. Farrell's the king-pin. It all turns around that merchant.'

Rodtem asked, 'We take some men with us?'

Bassett turned, looked at his bunkhouse. He scowled and rubbed his jaw. Finally his decision was made.

'Us two. That's enough. No farmers in town, so Stuart said; that leaves Farrell alone.'

Rodtem said, 'How much?'

Bassett said, 'You draw good wages.'

Rodtem shook his head. 'A bonus,' he said. 'One hundred bucks.'

Bassett moved toward a bronc in a stall. 'Come along.' Rodtem showed his smile; he'd won. Bassett smoothed the heavy saddle-blanket on a sorrel, lifted his Miles City hull, screwed it down with a hard latigo. He got his rifle and broke it and saw the cartridge in the barrel. This slid into the saddle-holster, stock up.

Rodtem said, 'You're in a hurry, Ross.' He threaded his latigo, pulled, tied. By this time Ross Bassett was sitting his bronc in front of the barn, the late sunlight pale around horse and rider. Rodtem led his cayuse out and found his stirrup and lifted.

Bassett said, 'We'll make it by daylight yet.'

They loped toward Wild City, following the wagon-trail and its dust. Milt Stuart had come out of the cook-shack holding a cup and saucer, and now he watched the pair leave. The cook came to the door behind him and asked, 'Where's the boss an' Rodtem going?'

'Gun-fight, I think.'

'Yeah?'

'Down in Wild City.'

'Oh, yeah.'

Stuart said, 'By hades, I'm truthful. Farrell called him today when he organized his militia.'

The cook watched them ride. 'Maybe we oughta foller him, huh? Get some boys an' trail in?'

'Did he order it that way?'

The cook shot him a hard glance. He looked back at Bassett and Rodtem. 'No, he didn't; had he wanted us—he'd've so ordered it.' The cook went back into his kitchen. Stuart stood there, then went inside.

Sweat ran across their broncs, and dust gathered in it. They rode at a lope, running against the sun, and the sun didn't care. They forded the river, and Rodtem asked, 'What's the deal, boss?'

Now ponies fell to a grateful walk. Ross Bassett was thick in the saddle. 'I come down the street, and you watch from the side. You take your rifle. I'll ride in alone—on the main street, that is.'

'I'll come through the alley?'

Bassett said surlily, 'You guess fast!'

Rodtem was silent. He leaned back, his hands hooked around his horn; he looked at the sky and watched it. He said, 'No clouds; never no clouds.' But that didn't fit in. It had no place here.

Bassett spoke again. 'You watch from the side. If it gets too much for me, swing your rifle. Or if a farmer sides him, let the farmer have it. This is dog-eat-dog and use your fangs.'

Rodtem fingered his lip. 'I don't cotton to him.'

'Here's your chance.'

Rodtem nodded, very soberly.

Bassett looked at the sun and said, 'Dusk when we hit Wild City.' His hooks found his bronc and the animal found his lope again.

'Wish I had a drink, Bassett.'

'No whiskey until it's over with.'

'I still wish I had a drink.'

Bassett had no answer. He was looking back at the foothills and thinking, Redden is buried there, and nobody knows but me. He did not know why he thought of Slim Redden. Redden had worn out his allotment of days and knew the sun no more. And so it was.

He pulled his gaze down and looked at the house of a farmer, about a mile away. That log house, he decided, would make a good line-camp. He ran over this again, feeling for weak spots: with Farrell gone, the farmers would leave. Their general would be dead. What would a militia be without a leader? When he got done with this, he'd raid a farmhouse or two, and do some burning. Then, unorganized, the sodmen would leave.

Or else they could cross the river on Milo Dawson's grass . . . Dawson loved them, or so it seemed: he worked with them now. Bassett found this thought ironical, and wondered what Dawson would do after Wild City and Farrell were through. Then he knew he was thinking too far ahead; he pulled a screen across his mind, shutting out all thoughts except the corner reserved for Jack Farrell.

'Wild City,' Rodtem said.

Bassett said, 'Hold up horses.' They were at the mouth of an alley. 'A good man always looks over the road ahead.' He went down and Rodtem followed, and they left their horses soil-tied and walked into the alley. They went between two buildings, the narrow space so tight it dragged against them. Bassett looked at the main street, said, 'No farmers' rigs. That means no farmers.'

There were only the street and its dust, and the falling sun lying across it, giving it brightness, painting it red and yellow and blue. They went back into the alley.

Rodtem said, 'I lead our broncs down here, Ross. Then I slip in between the Merc and that other building. When you come back, I'll have your bronc with me.'

'I'll give you five minutes.'

'Enough.'

Rodtem stopped, looked at a building. 'I saw something move there, Ross. Back of the medico's office. Looked like a kid, going in that slot between the drug-store and the saloon.'

Ross Bassett looked, grunted something. Rodtem said, 'There he is.' From here they could see the street in front of Doc's office. Billy Stebbins was walking there, barefooted and whistling. The whistle was off-tune and high.

Bassett said, 'That Stebbins boy.'

'He'll tell Farrell.'

Bassett looked at him. 'You're gettin' jumpy. What difference does it make?' He moved down the alley, pulling his holster high ahead so it hung under his hand on the front of his thigh. Rodtem watched Billy Stebbins enter the Merc. Jack Farrell was in his office and the kid slipped in, shutting the door.

'Ma can't hear us, can she, Jack?'

Jack looked at the front of his store where Mrs. Stebbins was cleaning a counter, bolts of

171

cloth around her. 'No, why?'

'Ross Bassett,' Billy said, breathing hard. 'Him an' Rodtem just rid into town. I was watchin' the back of Doc's office to make sure he kept his promise when I seen them.'

'Where are they?'

'Rodtem, he stayed in the alley. Bassett walked up the alley, heading for here. He was pullin' his gun around in front.'

Jack got to his feet. He put his fists on his desk and looked toward Mrs. Stebbins. His bottom lip wanted to twitch; he caught it.

'You go lock the back door. We don't want anybody sneakin' in from the rear. Then stay in the store. Don't tell your mother. I'll be in the front.'

'I'll get my rifle.'

'You stay away from that .22. Now do as I say or I'll whale the daylights out of you!'

Billy's boyish face was very pale. 'All right, Jack.'

The boy scurried into the back room and Jack Farrell stood there, looking around his store. He stood there for a full minute, looking at the interior of his store but not seeing it. The tremble left his mouth and fixed in his fingers. He looked at his .45, turned the cylinder slightly.

He went toward the front door. A customer came in, and the woman said, 'Hello, Jack,' but he did not answer. She looked at him and showed her surprise, and Mrs. Stebbins was surprised, too. He went out and closed the door behind him and saw that already Ross Bassett was coming up the street, moving against the dusk and the buildings. Jack stepped out, went to one side, and stopped opposite the corner of his Mercantile. And there he waited, and hoped.

The rough part was Rodtem, back of him in the alley. But he shut the man from his mind, ruling his coarseness and anger out, and decided to take one obstacle at a time. He went ahead a few feet and stopped, watching Ross Bassett.

Bassett moved past the barber-shop, coming ahead, taking his time. The barber saw him and looked out and saw Jack. He had a queer, stupid look on his long face. He stood there. He said nothing. He just watched.

A man came out of the café, stopped, toothpick bobbing. Then the toothpick steadied, drooped. He pulled back into the doorway. Behind him came the waitress and the cook and they watched.

Bassett kept on coming. Jack said finally, 'That's far enough.'

Bassett stopped then. He looked at Jack and he looked long and hard, and his lips moved but made no sounds.

Jack said, 'You made your boast, Bassett.' Was it his voice so dry and distant?

Bassett's lips made sounds now. 'That's

173

why I'm here.' He looked across the street, looking at the buildings there, but Jack did not look that way. They heard the hard sound of a small rifle. Bassett jerked his head back, and said, 'All right, Farrell.'

Neither spoke again.

Later Jack Farrell remembered he was thinking of Martha Dawson. For some reason the golden beauty of her hair broke into and became lost in the scarlet lick of gunpowder. He remembered the silence of the town, and how it was suddenly and rudely shattered.

Then his right leg was gone and he was down on his hands and knees. He knew he was bloody and broken. He remembered shooting, and he remembered thinking, as Ross Bassett's bullet broke ahead of his, He got in first shot. Then he was down, and he shot again.

Bassett said, 'Don't shoot!'

He stood there, sick and slumped. Jack held his pistol up, smoke idling from it. Bassett dropped his gun and it clattered to the dried plank-walk with a wooden sound.

Bassett repeated, 'Don't shoot . . .' Only this time he did not scream. Jack got one leg under him, went down again. Bassett put out his right hand. He felt for the building beside him.

Jack lay there, watching. The time seemed to run into years, the years into centuries. Actually only a few seconds had run past them. He watched, blood on him, a great sickness in him.

Bassett found the wall. He put both hands against it and his head went down, and it never came up again. For the cowman's knees gave and he went slowly, pushing against the rough siding. It scraped him and then he was down, lying along the base of the wall, lying silent.

Doc came running. 'Jack—'

Jack said, 'Go back. There's Rodtem, back in the alley.'

Doc said, 'The kid got him. Shot him through the shoulder with his .22. Rodtem is down. I jumped him, too.'

Jack said, 'Darn that Billy.' That was all, then.

*     *     *

Today there are many farms on Wild River Basin. They are green and well-tilled fields of wheat and corn and oats and rye. The Montana Pacific Railroad runs along the edge of the wild river with its whitecaps and mad whirlpools. The Montana Pacific follows the river into the mountain pass that eventually leads it to Great Falls, Montana.

But Wild City is no more.

Farrelltown is the name now.

There is a new Merc Store—made of brick—and high on its wall are two pictures.

175

One is a picture of a woman. She has corn-gold hair, her face is dignified and sweet.

The other is the picture of her husband, Jack Farrell.

Both are gone now.

The old Dawson ranch—the Rafter T—is now run by a young man also named Jack Farrell. He is the grandson of the man who brought the first farmers into Wild River.

The Bassett Triangle S is no more. After the death of Bassett a nephew came out from Chicago to claim the ranch. He was no cowman—he admitted that fact—and he sold the Triangle S cattle to Milo Dawson. Today Dawson sleeps eternally under the Montana soil he loved so well. The soil he fought to hold.

It is history now—written into the history of Montana: windblown and dim history. Many of the people living today in Wild River Basin have not even heard of the deadly Wild River War.

To them the name of Farrell is nothing more than the name of the grandson of the old Jack Farrell, who now runs the Merc. Some of them—the older ones—remember old Jack Farrell. They remember how he limped on his right leg.

Few know that that limp came from the bullet of a man named Ross Bassett.

And so the dust gathers.

And the shifting panorama moves and brings new days and new seasons and new years. But there are sections of Wild River that are no good for farming land.

There are the alkali beds that are along Alkali Creek.

And across these white, glistening beds of silvery alkali the winds play and sing and conjure devil-twists—those small tornado-like winds that arise out of nowhere, then whirl and leap for the sky, swirling upward the white powdery dust.

These devil-twists whirl and dance their wild untamed dance, and maybe they remember, for they knew the old Jack Farrell—the Jack Farrell who brought settlers to Wild River—and they witnessed the savage war known as the Wild River War.

But if they do know, if they do remember, they can never tell, for they have no tongue. And if they could talk, perhaps they would not speak.

Perhaps they would prefer to keep forever their eternal secret.

Photoset, printed and bound in Great Britain by REDWOOD BURN LIMITED, Trowbridge, Wiltshire